What readers are saying about *Awakening*:

"A beautiful, eloquently written story…light BDSM with A LOT of emotion and passion! You will NOT be disappointed."

—*J. Woodbridge*

"Brilliant, fantastically written, and left me wanting to read more. Thank you to an author that's not afraid to say it how it is. I could not recommended this book to all my friends more if I tried."

—*S. Phillips*

"Wow, such a moving, fascinating book. Well done…a must read for all."

—*Carly L.*

"This a beautiful story of two people lost in their own guilt and loss, and finding that, yes, they can love again, but also that there should be no shame or disgust in accepting our own deepest desires."

—*Cloressa O.*

"I'm hooked."

—*Tori*

"Finally! A well-told story that shows the characters' vulnerabilities and how they learned to trust and love again."

—*A. Hirsch*

"I love romance novels with an extra added spice, and this was perfect."

—*R. Simons*

"I devoured it. Fab fab fab. What more can I say!!"

—*Sam*

"Couldn't put the book down, loved it."

—Samantha K.

"I enjoyed it and read it in one day."

—K. Adams

"Erotic and well written—and believable. An excellent and hot read."

—Caro

"A romance novel with a twist of BDSM in a comfortable way."

—Sharon

"Sallinger sure does know how to make you feel that 'in love' feeling."

—A. Hoffman

"A sweet romance showing how two broken people can fix themselves, with some BDSM to boot."

—Jaz-zing

"I really loved this book!"

—Bieshia S.

"Entertaining, sexy, and steamy."

—Lolly

"A very sweet and sexy story."

—Geri

"An original and introspective story."

—Booklover

awakening

elene sallinger

sourcebooks
casablanca

Published by Sourcebooks Casablanca, an imprint of Sourcebooks, Inc., in
conjunction with Xcite Books
P.O. Box 4410, Naperville, Illinois 60567-4410
(630) 961-3900
Fax: (630) 961-2168
www.sourcebooks.com

Originally published in 2012 in the UK by Xcite Books Ltd.

Library of Congress Cataloging-in-Publication data is on file with the publisher.

Printed and bound in the United States of America.
VP 10 9 8 7 6 5 4 3 2 1

Chapter 1

CLAIRE RYAN PUSHED OPEN the door to Bibliophile and struggled to calm her racing heart. Once inside, she rushed over to a large, square table covered in the newest bestsellers and leaned heavily against it as she struggled to regain her balance. Squeezing her eyes shut, she breathed deeply and silently chanted, *In two, three, four. Out two, three, four. In two, three, four. Out two, three, four.* She continued the breathing exercises she'd read about in her latest Zen book as she fought the panic rushing through her veins.

Fifteen years. That's how long it had been since she'd done anything social by herself, and she wasn't sure if she was going to be able to do this. She'd waffled all day about whether to come before finally becoming thoroughly sick of herself. It was just a goddamn book club meeting. It wasn't like she was running the gauntlet. Well, not literally.

The last year had been spent in near isolation with only Chester, her Pit Bull Terrier, for company. She had no friends, she was estranged from her family, and her relationship of fourteen years had ended, leaving her alone. Claire had been determined to take the time to figure out what she was doing with her life, and the last year had been spent laying the foundation for living.

For the first few months, she'd fooled herself into believing that she was actually living. She worked, she ate, she read, she went to sleep, and she took care of Chester. That was it. That was the sum total of Claire's life for the last 365 days. Today was the anniversary of her breakup with Charlie. It was no coincidence that she'd chosen it to re-enter the living world.

Slowly, Claire felt her chest loosen and her breathing slow to normal. Once she was certain she wasn't going to pass out, she stood and smoothed her sweater down over her hips before standing straight and taking one last deep breath. On the exhale, she finally took a look around the store.

Bibliophile was a small, local bookstore that catered to hardcore readers. It offered services for locating hard to find and out-of-print books and held regular readings, book clubs, and author events. For over ten years, Claire had walked by the store but never once been inside. She'd done all of her shopping at the local Barnes & Noble, online, or simply checked books out at the library.

The store was actually a converted town house in the growing urban district of River Rock, Vermont. It was cozy, with row upon row of shelves housing books of every genre. The front of the building was dominated by a huge bay window with a clever display of books set up like a house of cards. A sign announcing the store's monthly event calendar shared the space. Perpendicular to the window was the checkout counter, which held a smattering of pens and bookmarks along with a Dell flat-screen monitor and computer. The counter was neat and free of the usual clutter one tended to find in such places. In fact, as Claire scanned the store in search of the club meeting, it was neat as a pin. The floors were oak done in a parquet style where the grain alternated direction. Cheery yellow paint covered the walls, which were lined with classic movie posters and playbills. The overall effect was modern vintage.

Hearing voices coming from the back, Claire headed in that direction. Just as she stepped into the aisle between New Releases and Popular Fiction, a tall, darkly handsome man stepped out of the row closest to the register and walked behind the counter. That fast she lost her breath all over again.

He was tall, well over six feet, with close-cropped, black hair that showed just a hint of gray at the temples. His face was almost harsh, with a strong chin and straight nose. Given the heavy shadow he was sporting at just past 6:00 p.m., Claire guessed he probably had to shave twice a day if he really wanted to stay smooth. He was older, probably in his late forties, but extremely fit. His lean, firm body was accentuated by the black T-shirt and black jeans he wore. The T-shirt lovingly accentuated his broad shoulders and narrow waist. Rugged. That was it. If she had to find one word to describe him, it was rugged. He had her body tightening in places she'd forgotten about.

Claire watched as he set down the stack of books he was carrying and reached for the mouse. She felt rooted to the spot. She knew better than to gawk, but he was magnetic. She could stand there and watch him forever. He moved with an unconscious grace that was almost erotic.

His fingers were long and his hands were large yet surprisingly deft as he moved the mouse, clicking every now and then. From her angle, Claire could see that his eyes were a dark brown, and she bet that if she got close, she'd probably have a hard time discerning the iris from the pupil. He mesmerized her. She couldn't remember ever being so taken aback by a man. Not even Charlie, and he was the best looking man she'd ever dated.

Pain stabbed through her at the thought of Charlie. She had no right to stand there and ogle this man. After what she'd done, she knew better than to indulge in such a pointless endeavor. In obvious approval of her decision, a wave of cool air swept across Claire as a bell rung and another patron entered. The breeze fluttered her hair and pushed her gently toward the back. Taking it as a sign, Claire scurried into the stacks to find her club meeting.

"My biggest issue was that this was more book porn than romance. I mean, the author used the c-word relentlessly and they were always doing it. It was a real turn-off," the woman said for what had to be the fifth time. Inside, Claire couldn't help but wonder at the paradox between her appearance and her prudish sensibility. She was rail thin, with bottle black hair, deep red lipstick, and a sparkling silver chain connecting the hoops in her upper lip and outer eyebrow. If anything, Claire would have been expecting her to champion the carnality of the book. It was judgmental, she knew, but there you have it.

"Book porn. Hardly," scoffed the club moderator, a slim, middle-aged woman with long, blond hair pulled back in a simple ponytail that hung down her back. "Book porn has no plot. It has no conflict or crisis. It has no character development. It simply jolts from one sex scene to the next. This had it all. The characters were well drawn. The plot was involved. The sex was graphic, admittedly, but given the fact that the main character was a vampire assassin, I think it was appropriate." She punctuated each phrase with large, round gestures as she warmed up to the topic.

Claire tuned out again at this point. She'd been only half listening to the discussion and she hadn't been participating other than the one time the moderator had deliberately attempted to draw her into the conversation by asking her which of the book's characters was her favorite. Thank God she'd actually read the book. It was J. R. Ward's *Dark Lover*, and Claire had absolutely loved the story. She was already well into book two, but after that one answer Claire had only been halfheartedly tuned into the discussion.

It wasn't that she had a problem with the group; she just had never been much of a joiner. She'd chosen this particular club because the one and only thing she had consistently done over the last several years was read romance novels. It had been the only outlet for her frustrated desire for sex. And, in the year since she and Charlie split, she'd read so many romance novels she'd run out of space on her shelves and had maxed her Nook's memory out twice. It had made logical sense to join a book club for romance readers. She figured she'd come out, maybe see if she could meet some nice, like-minded people, and just force herself to be around humans at least once a week. She wasn't particularly optimistic, but she'd vowed to attend at least four meetings before giving up.

The group was an eclectic mix of young and older women. There was one lone man in the group, though Claire suspected he was gay. Unlike most gatherings of people, this group was very participative and she was sure she was coming off like a wallflower, but she just didn't have it in her yet to really participate. It was a lot for her to even be at the meeting. What she really wanted to do was get up and browse the store. It had been so long since she'd been inside a real bookstore and not a revolving book warehouse, she'd forgotten what a sensory experience it was. Colorful book jackets tantalized her, and the smell of paper, ink, and coffee made her want to wallow in them. Bibliophile was riding the trend of the twenty-first century bookshop and had coffee and snacks available. The sharp, chocolaty aroma of the brew was making Claire's mouth water, and it looked like chocolate chip cookies to boot, but she could be patient until the meeting broke for refreshments.

Unlike the large, faceless chains with their impersonal cafes, Mr. Rugged from the front of the store had made several pots of coffee during the meeting and stocked out muffins and cookies. There was a small, clear acrylic tin on the side table where everything was neatly arranged asking for donations to the coffee fund, and even from her seat across the meeting area, Claire could see that it was stuffed full of bills and coins.

The area where they were meeting was cozy, with a large rug and a low coffee table surrounded by big, overstuffed armchairs and plenty of folding ones to accommodate the group members. Claire suspected that if she came back when there were no meetings, just the table and armchairs would be in the center, as neatly arranged as the rest of the store.

"Okay, everyone. Great meeting. Next time, it's *The Devil Who Tamed Her* by Johanna Lindsey. Evan has been kind enough to offer a 20 percent discount to all club members on their purchases, so don't forget to register at the front." The moderator stood up, signaling an end to the meeting.

Claire stood and started to make good her escape, only to be thwarted by her.

"Hi there." She held out a slim, well-toned arm. "I'm Jean. We didn't get a chance to meet before the meeting started. It's always good to have a new member and I wanted to be sure to welcome you."

"Thank you. I'm Claire," she said a bit awkwardly as she shook Jean's hand. The woman's grip was firm and warm. It had been so long since she'd had to interact socially that she didn't really know how to continue. "I'm sorry I didn't really join in that much, I..." She shrugged as she ran out of anything to say that wouldn't force her to lie to the woman.

"Oh"—Jean waved a dismissive hand—"no worries. You'll warm up to us. We tend to be very vocal, and after a while you won't be able to resist us." She grinned widely.

"Well, I have to get home. My husband will be waiting for me. We'll see you next time, right?" She looked at Claire with a quirked eyebrow.

"Yes," Claire said with a definitive nod. She would tough this out.

"Good." She patted Claire's arm as she moved off, calling over her shoulder, "Next time, you'll lead the discussion."

Claire stiffened and her eyes widened. "What! Oh no. Jean, wait." She started off after her, only to stop up short as she stubbed her toe on the coffee table. "Dammit!" she muttered as she plopped down into the nearest seat and hugged her abused toe into her lap. Thank God for the boots she was wearing, otherwise she was willing to bet she'd have broken it.

"Shit," she grumbled under her breath. She'd wanted to ease

back into socializing, not get booted into the spotlight. She'd just have to talk with Jean about this next week. Right now, the coffee was calling her and she wanted to pick up some new books, including the club's next selection.

Claire wandered Bibliophile browsing the various aisles and acquainting herself with the layout. Her fingers danced along the colorful spines the way children ran their fingers along the pickets of a fence as she absorbed the swish of the book jackets under her touch and her eyes swam with the colors and type. She was waiting for that spark, that hint saying *this one*. She felt the overwhelming need to connect to something, anything. She'd been alone for a long time now with just her books and her dog and she was tired of her own company. Surely one year completely alone was sufficient penance. Surely she could try to find a friend if nothing else.

The fourteen years she'd spent with Charlie represented the absolute worst experience of her life. The relationship had been abusive on so many levels, and she hadn't found enough scalding water to cleanse her soul of her crimes. She'd put him through the worst kind of hell and she'd done it willfully. When he'd finally left her, the biggest relief had been knowing that she couldn't hurt him anymore.

At first, she'd been content to be by herself. She'd recognized that the world didn't deserve her baggage. She was never going to do to another human being what she'd done to Charlie. It wouldn't be fair to anyone. Watching someone slowly come to hate you was a chilling experience and one that haunted her. She had only to look in the mirror to see the evidence of his pain and she was determined to go it alone rather than take the risk of hurting anyone else.

Being alone was easier said than done. She'd made it through the year she had vowed to do, but now there were some days where simply breathing hurt. Everything about her life was isolated. She lived by herself and didn't know her neighbors. Her only companionship was Chester, and as much as she loved him, he couldn't talk to her. Her work as a diamond grader and jewelry appraiser was solitary, and she could go days without interacting with a single coworker beyond the perfunctory communication necessary to perform the work. She was no longer just alone, she was profoundly lonely. Hence, the book club. She needed human interaction.

Claire continued along the last aisle spanning the wall at the front of the store until she found what she was looking for, the Romance section. She quickly scanned the author last names until she found *L* and picked up the club's selection for the next meeting. That done, she scanned the titles and randomly picked up books from her favorite authors. As she reached for one paperback, a book on the next shelf over caught her eye. The title, *Finding Herself,* all but jumped up and smacked her on the face. Its large, bold script against a plain black book jacket fairly blinked *look at me, look at me.*

Claire picked up the book, flipped it over, and scanned the blurb, only to thrust the book right back onto the shelf and turn away. That wasn't a romance novel; it was an erotica anthology— about BDSM. She hadn't bothered to pay attention to the tag on the shelf indicating the genre. She wasn't interested in reading erotica; at least, that's what she was telling herself since her fingers were almost itching to pick that book back up.

Over the last year, her reading selections had become more and more risqué. She'd grown up on the likes of Barbara Cartland where there was no sex at all or, if there was, it was a discreet sentence where the heroine very pristinely offered up her virginity. During her relationship with Charlie, when sex became less and less frequent, and especially after it was nothing more than participatory masturbation, she'd begun to read progressively more sexually explicit novels.

J. R. Ward's *Brotherhood* series had been the answer to her dreams. Lots of graphic sex tied up into a love story. She'd masturbated a lot after reading one of those books. If you could call what she did masturbation. Applying steady pressure to her clit outside her panties didn't rank up there with what she'd heard of other women doing, but it got her off and that's all she really cared about. Racy romance novels were one thing, but erotica was something else entirely. But that blurb, it was as if it were seared into her brain. One sentence in particular had made her tingle…*Join us as these women submit to their secret desire to be ruled by that one man, the one who sees inside her and pushes her beyond her inhibitions to pleasures she's not even dared to fantasize about.*

Every cell in her body was screaming for her to buy that book. So many times she had wanted to ask Charlie to do something to her, only to be embarrassed and bite her tongue. So many times she had been frustrated at his tendency to just keep it simple and fuck her lying on their sides, rubbing her clit until she came, when what she really wanted was for him to get rough and fuck her like he couldn't breathe if he didn't take her. She craved hot, jungle sex but had never had the courage to demand it. And truthfully, after a while, he'd only had sex with her because she was there and he wasn't a cheater. She didn't blame him for not putting any effort into it, but that didn't do anything about her frustrated desires.

Almost against her will, she found herself backtracking and pulling the anthology off the shelf. For long moments, she just stared at it. The cover was compelling. The image was in shadows and quite artistic. A naked woman knelt in profile with her hands behind her back, tied with what looked like a scarf. Her nipples were hard and her lips were parted. She was blindfolded and her head was bent. Her posture epitomized supplication, but her arousal was obvious. Claire gripped the book so hard her knuckles showed white. She wanted to read it, but she was nervous. What if it was really perverted? Imagining what might be inside those pages, however, had her breath hitching just a bit and a slow flush sweeping through her limbs.

Claire darted a glance toward the front of the store where the cash register was located. There was no way she was going to walk up to Mr. Rugged and ring that book out. That was like having to buy tampons or yeast infection medicine and the only cashier in the store was a gorgeous guy. She couldn't do it. She might not be willing to talk to him, but she damn sure wasn't going to embarrass herself in front of him.

With a sigh, she started to put the book back, only to stop abruptly as she caught sight of Mr. Rugged rearranging the armchairs in the reading area. The flex and flow of his muscles as he moved made her palms itch to touch him. He didn't notice her perusal as he took the last two folding chairs into what had to be a store room in the back corner, leaving the four leather club chairs as Claire had imagined they would be—perfectly lined up, one at each edge of the low, square coffee table.

Tingles flew through her body as the idea overtook her. She could read it here. Bibliophile catered to readers. It was encouraged even. She'd just spend some time reading a few of the selections and make sure she put it back before she left. She didn't have to buy it, and she didn't even have to feel guilty because she was going to buy several books before she left.

Decision made, Claire slipped the book into her stack and headed back to the reading area. Settling into the furthest chair from the front, she set her intended purchases on the table and flipped to the first story.

Chapter 2

EVAN LANE STEPPED OUT of the stacks leading to the back of the store and stopped short as he saw the newest member of the Romance Readers Book Club settled into one of the leather club chairs and engrossed in whatever it was she was reading. Her long, honey-brown hair hung like a satin curtain hiding her face, but as he watched, she tucked the hair on the side closest to him behind one ear, giving him a tantalizing view of clear, creamy skin, elegant cheekbones, and delicate features. She was so small only her head was visible over the top of the chair, but Evan already knew what she looked like from the neck down. Petite, with a trim frame and small, pert breasts encased in a simple, pale green sweater and form-fitting blue jeans. She wore high-heeled leather boots that gave her a few inches in height, but he was willing to bet she barely reached his chin without the heels.

He'd been surreptitiously watching her since he first saw her walk in and grab the display table like her life depended on it. She seemed so delicate and skittish, as if she'd run at a moment's notice. His first instinct had been to go to her and make sure she was OK. His breath had caught at the sight of her and his stomach had lurched, which had made no sense, but then, when she grabbed the table, he'd understood. He had obviously sensed her distress.

Evan considered himself a fairly empathetic man. He liked to believe he was tuned into other people and able to sense intuitively what they might need. It was a quality that had served him well over the years. Her fragility had called to him the moment he'd seen her. But, unless she passed out in the middle of his store, he was leaving her alone.

He needed to clean up the coffee area and put away the snacks in preparation for closing, but that was going to put him right behind her and part of him wanted to stay as far away from her as possible. The entire time she'd been in the store, he'd made sure to be at the opposite end. She made him twitchy, like ants were crawling under his skin. It was almost as if she were dangerous. Which, of course, made no sense. She was simply a customer and a small, fragile-looking one at that. Hell, she probably didn't weigh more than a hundred pounds soaking wet and, God knew, she couldn't actually harm him, so this weirdness really needed to end. With a decisive shake of his head, Evan moved over to the coffee area and began emptying out the filter and wiping away crumbs.

Evan wasn't trying to compete with the Barnes & Nobles and Amazons of the world. He simply wanted to offer dedicated readers a place to come where they could find unusual selections and enjoy the atmosphere while reading a good book. Bibliophile had been his dream since he was a teenager. He'd always been bookish but had wanted to get out of the small, podunk town he'd been raised in, so he'd joined the military and never looked back.

After spending sufficient time in the service to have racked up several combat tours, multiple injuries, and enough nightmares to last a lifetime, he'd been honorably discharged and had opened Bibliophile. It was the culmination of his dream and he loved every minute of building and running the store. Bibliophile was really the only thing that kept him going after…*No!* He wasn't going there. He took a deep, steadying breath and resumed his task until everything was arranged to his satisfaction.

Turning, he planned to remind the woman that closing time was in thirty minutes; however, the sight she made knocked the wind out of him. The book she was reading was open in her lap and she gripped the edges as if she'd fight anyone who tried to prevent her from reading it. Her lips were parted and her breathing was ragged.

Before he could ask if something was wrong, she brought one hand to her chest, pressing in hard as if to steady herself, and that's when he noticed. Her nipples were hard, jutting out in stark relief from behind the thin knit of her sweater. He'd noted before that her legs were crossed, but now he saw she was clamping them together viciously. She was excited.

Whatever she was reading, she was aroused. There was an empty book jacket lying on the table, and a quick glance at the book in her hands confirmed that she'd removed the cover. It was upside down, but Evan was intimately acquainted with his stock and he knew that cover. It was *Finding Herself*, she was reading dominance and submission erotica, and if her body language was any indication, she was close to coming.

Evan's body reacted violently to the knowledge. His cock punched into an erection straining mightily behind his zipper and his chest clenched hard as what breath he had left dissolved in his lungs. He fell back against the coffee bar, hard enough to rattle the contents, and she jumped as if she'd been shocked. Whipping her head around, she gazed up at him with wide, glossy hazel eyes. Her pupils were dilated and her cheeks were dusted pink with the flush of arousal. Evan's cock twitched hard and he felt himself beginning to leak. Horror shot through him. No *fucking* way. This wasn't happening.

Before he could stop himself, he pushed off the coffee bar and growled out, "We close in thirty minutes. You'll need to check out." He stalked off toward the front, ignoring the flush of humiliation that stained her cheeks as he left her there.

~~~

Claire felt the color burning her skin as if it were a brand. She cringed with the humiliation of Mr. Rugged having seen her in that state. She'd almost climaxed just from reading the story. In truth, she'd been considering finding the bathroom and taking care of herself.

It reminded her of the time she had gone over to her friend Katie Shannon's house for a slumber party. Katie had found her father's porn stash and they'd watched a video after he'd gone to bed. It had been very mundane in retrospect, just a whole lot of rough doggy style, but Claire had been so affected by the video, she'd had to go into the bathroom to relieve the tension. When she was done, she'd gone back out, but the video had been over.

She'd never forgotten that movie. Oscar-worthy cinematography it was not, but it had still changed her life. She'd used it as fodder for her burgeoning fantasies for many months until she'd discovered romance novels. It remained the only porn she'd ever seen. Reading this book had been almost like that. Oh, her physical reaction had been exactly the same, but that story had resonated with her in ways she didn't quite understand.

The story was quite simple. Carol, a woman recently separated from her lover, finds herself being dragged to a local sex club by her best friend. There she meets a man who tempts her with promises of sensations and experiences she's never had before if she agrees to follow his every instruction. The woman agrees and proceeds to submit to the man's every whim.

Reading it had been like feeling as if layers of her psyche she hadn't even known existed were being unwrapped. She felt exposed and somehow vulnerable. She'd expected to start the book, get hit by some graphic, deviant sex, and then put it down. Curiosity satisfied. Instead, it had been as if the book were glued to her hands. As if she were drowning and that book was her lifeline. She could no more have put it down without finishing that story than she could have told her heart not to beat.

Everything faded as the words painted erotic images in her mind. She lost track of her surroundings, of the very time passing. Claire had been drenched and on edge within the first five pages, and she'd been hovering on the brink of climax throughout every paragraph since Sir had told Carol to strip for him.

Claire had literally begun to ache. Her nipples had hardened and she'd flooded her panties. She'd always wanted to have rough, animalistic sex, but she'd never considered submitting to anyone so completely. She didn't see herself as submissive. But she did want something more than your garden variety sex. To this day, she dreamed of having her lover grab her and have his way with her. Making love to her as if his life depended on getting deep inside her and fucking her senseless.

She couldn't remember a single time in her life where she hadn't had to resort to the fantasy of rough sex in order to have an orgasm. She couldn't relate to the romance novels she read where women got so caught up in the moment with their lover that all it took was sensation alone to make them climax. She'd always wondered if something was wrong with her because not once in her entire sexual experience had she ever been so lost in sensation or caught up in the moment that the grocery list or some other chore wasn't running through her head.

She couldn't even get away with faking an orgasm, because Charlie wouldn't let her. He wouldn't come until she did, but she'd always had to be the one to ratchet the tempo up between her and Charlie and she'd always felt foolish doing so. Over time, she'd grown to dislike gentle sex, and it was the only kind she'd had for the entirety of her adult life. Charlie was a skilled and attentive lover in the beginning of their relationship; after she'd betrayed him one time too many, he'd been a bystander just lying there while she rutted over him to get them both off. Or just sticking it in and pumping for his own gratification. Her orgasm had become her sole responsibility.

After a while, it was easier just to suck him off and take care of her own business in the shower where she didn't have to face his silent resentment during such an intimate act. It had taken fourteen years for her to get up the courage to finally give him his freedom.

But, oh my God, she'd almost come just from reading the words. She literally had been so caught up that she'd forgotten everything around her. It was as if she'd become Carol and it had been Claire submitting to Sir. She shivered as tendrils of sensation whispered through her at the memory of his domination. But, just her luck, Mr. Rugged had witnessed her arousal and obviously been disgusted by her. It didn't take a genius to figure out what her ragged breathing and hard nipples meant. Claire just prayed he didn't know which book she'd been reading.

Remembering his brusque admonishment to check out, her cheeks flamed again. She'd go ahead and buy the books, since she'd spent several hours taking up space in his store, but it looked like she'd have to find another club. There was no way she was coming back here.

Evan sat rigidly behind the counter waiting for the woman to come and buy her books. He'd already straightened up the front tables and begun the nightly paperwork. Now, if only his goddamned dick would cooperate he could calm down. He was disgusted with himself. Getting a fucking hard-on like he was a teenager at the sight of a woman's erect nipples. What the hell was wrong with him? OK, so he hadn't been with a woman since Marianne had died, but so fucking what. He hadn't wanted to. It wasn't that he no longer had the urge; he just couldn't bring himself to be with some random woman or to take a casual lover. And what could this woman be to him, other than something casual? She wasn't Marianne. Enough said.

He'd tried once to be with a woman, about six months after Marianne died, and it had been a disaster for both of them. He hadn't even been able to get hard. He'd simply given her a session and used toys on her until she came. She'd asked to see him again, but he'd turned her away as diplomatically as possible and then proceeded to drink himself into a stupor to forget.

At first, it had been hard to go without sex. He'd get so horny he wouldn't be able to sit still, but it always ended the same way—he'd masturbate in the shower to images of Marianne and by the time his come was jetting the tears would be streaming. After a while, he just couldn't take the pain any longer. Now, he was just numb.

At least, he had been until tonight. This was the first spontaneous erection he'd had in the two years since her death, but what he and Marianne had shared had been soul deep and, having had that, he didn't want a poor substitute who would only remind him of how empty he already was without her.

Marianne had been his wife, his lover, his soul mate, and his submissive for ten years before she'd died of ovarian cancer. Evan had known the moment he'd met her that she was going to be his. She had taken a bit more convincing. She was a fiery and fiercely independent woman who had nonetheless taken to submitting to him like a duck to water once he'd dared her to stop being a coward and try it. Marianne had been a sucker for a dare.

Pain squeezed Evan's chest at the memories flooding his mind. He missed her so much. They were supposed to grow old together. He wasn't supposed to be here by himself. She wasn't supposed to abandon him. Evan's eyes burned and he clenched his teeth against the grief that threatened to well up. Evan took a deep breath and pushed memories of Marianne away. No time for that now.

He flicked a glance to the back of the store, but there was no sign of her. *Jesus!* What the hell was taking her so long? Evan just wanted her gone. He wanted her out of his store, and the sooner, the better. He stood up to go remind her, again, to check out, knocking his stool back and almost tipping it over in his haste to run her out of the store. By the time he'd righted the stool, however, she was there setting her books gently, almost hesitantly, on the counter without looking at him and then digging in her satchel for her wallet.

"Driver's license," he gritted out as he put out his hand palm up. *About damn time.*

"Huh?" She looked up, flushing slightly as she met his gaze. Delicately arched brows crinkled over her large, hazel eyes. "I'm sorry, why do you need my driver's license?" Her voice was soft, tentative almost, but with a smoky, deep quality. It rubbed his skin like silk and he gritted his teeth in aggravation.

"For the discount. For the book club." His tone all but screamed "Duh!" and he knew he was being rude, but he didn't seem able to help himself. He wanted her gone.

"Oh, um, no thanks." She shook her head, sending the honey-brown curtain swinging, and waved a dismissive hand. "There's no need." She flushed deeper and looked back down into her satchel where she appeared to finally locate her wallet and pulled it out.

"What do you mean?" he snapped. "You're a member of the book club. You're buying the next book for discussion"—he pointed to the paperback on the top of the stack—"and I gave my word that all members would get the discount. Now, your driver's license, please, so I can put you into the system."

"No, really. It isn't necessary. Please just ring me out and I'll be on my way." She seemed to flush even deeper, if that were possible. She also seemed to be very fixated on a spot over his shoulder since she was refusing to look at him.

"Look, lady. I'm not having Jean down my back because I didn't keep my word." He glared at her. The rational part of his brain was screaming at him to calm down and stop acting like an ass, but the air conditioning had kicked on and he could smell her now. Her light, floral scent whispered across his nose and his dick had just rejoined the party. It was taking immense self-control not to reach in and adjust himself.

Rather than hand over her ID, she took a step back from the counter, squeezed her eyes shut, and took several deep breaths, which, of course, meant Evan was once again staring at her tits. *Aaaaaaaah!* The mental scream resonated around his brain like an echo. He didn't understand where this anger was coming from. It wasn't like him to be this undisciplined.

She opened her eyes, lifted her chin, and met his glare. "I won't be back, so don't worry about it. Now, please ring me up or I can just leave the books here."

A flash of panic surged through Evan, followed closely by shame. Not coming back? He wanted her to leave, yes, he needed some breathing room. He wasn't trying to run her away for good. Evan prided himself on providing a friendly environment and he had a large number of loyal customers. Her hazel gaze never wavered, though; she meant it.

On the heels of that realization, as if a pin had been pushed into a balloon, his anger deflated, leaving him cold and embarrassed by his behavior. Taking a deep, deep breath and blowing it out, Evan closed his eyes for a moment, before looking at her once again.

"Look, I'm sorry."

"Huh?" She scowled. His apology had clearly not been what she was expecting.

Evan blew out another deep breath. "I apologize for my rudeness. It's been, well, it's been a very trying night for me, but I'm taking it out on you and I apologize for that." He pulled his stool closer and sat down in an effort to relax. "Please, don't let my stupidity keep you from coming back. I'm not the asshole I'm pretending to be right now. I just…Well, I'm sorry."

"Pretending? If that's an act, you should be on stage." Evan barked a laugh at that and she smirked at him. Not so meek after all.

"OK." He smiled at her then. "You got me there. Will you please let me process your membership and come back next week? If I have to tell Jean that you didn't come back because of me, she'll have my hide."

Her face fell and she shook her head. "That's OK. I'm not sure it's the right place for me. Besides, she won't even know I'm gone. I barely participated."

"Oh, she'll know. Jean is like a mother hen. Once someone steps through those doors for her club, they are indelibly marked in her brain. She knows every member and remembers every dropout. So, please, let me?"

She stared at him for several moments with narrowed eyes. Evan could imagine the wheels turning in her mind, but finally she just nodded once—a sharp, quick movement of her head—and dug out her ID, which she handed to him, being very careful not to touch his skin.

Another flash of shame shot through him. He'd really succeeded in being an ass tonight. Marianne would've been so disappointed in him. Grief surged through him again and he ruthlessly shoved it down and began to type in her contact information. Once he'd set up her account and rung out her books, he placed the receipt in her bag and handed it to her.

"Thank you, Ms. Ryan. I mean that. You really saved me." He tried for a smile, but it felt more like a grimace.

"Right." She smirked again, her tone faintly sarcastic.

"Will you be back?" he called after her as she headed for the door. He'd meant every word he'd said about Jean. He did not want to piss her off.

"Yessir." It was said in the offhand way people do when they aren't really thinking about their response and they don't know the person well enough to address them by name, but Evan's body didn't care. All it heard was "Sir" and he felt his cock start to leak.

Mo-ther-fuck-er!

"Evan," he growled. "Evan, not Sir."

She stopped with her hand on the door at his tone. Her eyes snapped to his and widened at whatever she saw there. Quirking her head to the side, she contemplated him for a few moments before narrowing her eyes again. "Yes…Evan…I'll be back."

Without another look his way, she left the store. A sharp, stabbing pain shot up his arm and Evan looked down to see the pencil he'd been holding was now splintered and digging into his palm.

Fuck.

Chapter 3

FRAGRANT RIBBONS OF STEAM curled around Claire as she drifted in the tub. This was one of her favorite activities, but not one she indulged in often. She kept her life very scheduled, and a leisurely soak in the tub generally didn't fit into that category. Tonight, though, she felt too edgy, too out of sorts. It was as if an electrical current was running under her skin and she couldn't relax. So, instead of her usual efficient shower, she was now soaking in her tub in her darkened bathroom lit only with melon-scented candles. She'd added a few drops of almond oil to the water and the silky heat was soothing, but that edge was still there.

It definitely wasn't the atmosphere that was preventing her from relaxing. She'd spent a lot of time on her bathroom to get it just right. She'd always wanted a bathroom that felt like a spa. The walls were a delicate blue with white wainscoting. Her tub was a vintage claw-foot model in white and was tucked into the alcove formed by the bay window and had shelving installed at either end for her candles and jars of oil. When she did soak, she liked to crack the wooden shade to gaze at the night sky or to cloud watch, depending on the time of day. The rest of the bathroom was functional and efficient, with a separate shower tucked into one corner. A white vanity and large mirror took up the wall opposite the tub. White tile and stainless steel fixtures rounded out the decor. She was neat by nature and didn't like clutter, so the only things on top of her vanity were her toothbrush and toothpaste and a bottle of soap. Everything else was efficiently organized in bins and baskets under the sink.

She knew what was going on; she just didn't want to face it. Ever since she'd read that story in *Finding Herself* it had been as if she had ants under her skin. She'd also stayed aroused. Her jeans had rubbed against her the entire walk home. Once inside, she'd changed into some sweats just to relieve the pressure before letting Chester out of his crate. To make matters worse, as if she weren't uncomfortable enough, he'd barreled into her and shoved his face into her crotch before quirking his head and looking up at her inquiringly. How embarrassing that the dog she'd had for two years had never scented sexual arousal on her, making it a new scent that needed cataloguing. She'd pushed him away and made him sit, but it had embarrassed her nonetheless.

After walking Chester and dealing with the usual nasty looks she got every time she took her Pit Bull Terrier out in the little urban, artsy community she lived in, she'd come home and fixed a simple garden salad and a glass of Sangria for dinner. As she ate, she'd reflected on the exchange with Bibliophile's owner. She didn't understand why he'd asked her to come back after being so obviously disgusted with her. She'd meant it when she'd said she had no intention of returning to the store. She was mortified at her behavior and humiliated at his having witnessed it. He'd seemed sincere, though. At least, she'd thought he'd gotten over whatever the issue was until she'd called him Sir. Then he'd acted as if she'd stabbed him with a hot poker.

She'd really loved the store, though. And she wanted to go back. It was cozy and the atmosphere was so welcoming—well, if you left Mr. Rugged, make that Evan, out of the picture. The reading area just screamed *make yourself at home* and the coffee had been excellent. She'd ended up losing complete track of the time and that had been due just as much to the setting as it had been to the story. Hell, it was a free country and sooner or later she was going to have to start living her own life. With a nod, Claire decided she'd go back one more time and see how things went.

None of these ruminations, however, helped her get past her tension. Her muscles were beginning to ache. She'd finally given up on relaxing without intervention and had turned to the tub. Usually a soak relaxed her to the point of nodding off, but no such luck tonight. Tonight, her body had other ideas.

At the moment, her dilemma was that she couldn't wait any longer, but she didn't usually masturbate like this and she was uncomfortable. The story had been so graphic and detailed. Carol's body had been catalogued in its texture and taste and, frankly, Claire wondered if any of it was true. She had never read such graphic descriptions and she certainly had never touched herself directly. Well, she'd done it when Charlie had demanded it, but that had been for his pleasure, not her own, and had just been quick little flicks of her clit until he took over.

When she wanted to come on her own, she performed the same ritual she'd been performing since she'd first discovered orgasm. She lay face down on her bed and reached between her legs, being careful to keep to the outside of her panties. She then located her clit under its hood and simply pressed until she came. She would fantasize in order to speed up the process, but her fantasies were pretty sedate, featuring nothing more than straight-up, doggy style sex where the guy was overwhelmed by his attraction for her and simply had to have her. The only variable in her fantasy was the man. Sometimes it was a security guard, sometimes a cop who pulled her over, sometimes an imaginary step-relative, and sometimes an imaginary husband. But only the imaginary face changed; everything else remained the same. She'd been masturbating the exact same way for years.

After having read that short story, however, she was wondering exactly how much she'd been shorting herself. She'd never really pondered why she didn't touch herself directly, but now she was. She didn't enjoy her body very much. She didn't like the way she looked at all. She might be on the slim side, but she was definitely pear shaped and her breasts were so small she could get by without wearing a bra if she chose. She wore one, just to give herself a bit of shape, and the padding helped balance her out a bit. When she'd had short hair she'd been mistaken for a boy whenever she wore baggy clothes. No, not very flattering at all. As for not going near the coochie unless Charlie directed her to, she didn't really know the answer to that; she only knew that she didn't. She never had. It seemed dirty, messy even.

Her hands clenched along the sides of her tub. She almost vibrated with the need for release. Her nipples were hard where they poked out from the water and, as much as she'd like to claim it was from the evaporation, it was because she was horny. Her intimate muscles were clenched in a never-ending Kegel and the jittery feeling that had started in the bookstore was only growing worse.

Come on, Claire. You promised no more self-delusion. Do you want to know or don't you?

Bottom line…She wanted to know.

Evan glared at the bottle of whiskey as if it had stolen his wallet and wouldn't give it back. He was currently sprawled out on his couch with his feet propped up on the vintage footlocker that he used as a coffee table/storage bin. The fifth of Evan Williams, no relation, was next to his foot, a silent sentry in his war to lose himself in liquid oblivion.

He'd moved into the apartment over the top of Bibliophile after Marianne died. He simply couldn't stay in their brownstone. Marianne had decorated every inch of their home and it had been like ripping out stitches every time he'd walked through the door.

So, as soon as his tenant's lease was up, he'd moved in. The small, one-bedroom apartment suited his purposes and was enough for him. It had been especially helpful as he'd begun to spend more and more time at the shop. Rather than driving across town, he just went out the back door and up the stairs.

He hadn't brought a single piece of furniture with him from the brownstone. He'd sold everything in the house and had gone out and bought himself a sectional in weathered, brown leather and the footlocker for his feet. He'd put a simple birch platform bed, dresser, and nightstand in the bedroom and rounded out his "I don't give a fuck" decor with a small, wooden dinette that doubled as his desk when he worked on his laptop.

Evan was an aesthete at heart, though, and over time art had bloomed on the walls when something caught his fancy. A bookcase now adorned the back wall and his favorite books were on display. And, since he was a huge proponent of lounging comfortably while watching his 42-inch flat-screen, a plush chenille throw in a creamy white draped over his sofa for when he really wanted to get cozy. He was comfortable with his apartment. Most importantly, he wasn't swarmed by memories every time he walked through the door. He'd left all visible reminders at the brownstone.

Well, not every single one. The photo albums Marianne had made for him were in the bookcase. Albeit on the lowest shelf in the farthest corner, where he really had to make a point of looking to see them, but they were there nonetheless. Tonight, they felt like a magnet. Drawing him. Taunting him. Daring him to walk the path of memory. Something he definitely wanted to avoid.

Which was where the whiskey came in. It was supposed to be dulling the ache. It wasn't helping and he was growing increasingly frustrated. He didn't want to think about Marianne tonight and he definitely didn't want to think about Her. The whiskey was supposed to drive all thoughts from his brain. It was his go-to solution on days like today, where everything was too raw, too close to the surface.

He wasn't an alcoholic, though it had been touch-and-go there after Marianne had passed. In fact, he rarely drank at all anymore; he generally didn't need it. The loneliness had sunk into his marrow, altering his DNA so that it was just a part of him now and not something to dwell on.

Tonight, though, all he saw was her, Claire Ryan. He should have let her leave, then he wouldn't know her name, the fact that she lived five blocks down the street, was five feet, three inches tall, weighed 115 pounds, and had opted to be an organ donor. Damn driver's license. If he'd let her go, she just be another nameless customer who might or might not walk back through his door. But what she wouldn't be was this persistent itch under his skin.

He never lost his temper. He prided himself on his restraint and discipline. It had been essential in the military and it had been even more so in his relationship, but he'd behaved like a complete ass tonight. It was bad enough his body had forgotten he was a grown man and not a teenager who'd never seen tits before, but to literally be standing there dripping simply because she called him Sir, unintentionally at that, was too much to deal with. It had been so long since he'd had any kind of release he'd almost forgotten what an erection felt like, but clearly his body was waking up and it was damned unwelcome.

Blowing out a hard breath, Evan got up, pulled the red leather album from the shelf, and brought it back to the couch. Marianne had been a secret crafter; she didn't make a production out of it, but she loved to hand make gifts for people. This particular album was one she'd taken special care with. It was her gift to him on the first anniversary of her submission to him.

The photos were artistic and highly erotic. She'd taken the vast majority of them by herself, posing for various shots in the ways he demanded when they were together. He'd loved for her to be corseted and on her knees waiting for him, her head bowed. She'd captured that moment perfectly. Another favorite was watching her masturbate. He'd be close enough to smell her arousal as she fingered herself or went to town with a dildo. Each one of those moments was captured in black and white, giving them a haunted mystery that was so reflective of Marianne in the depths of her submission.

She was a joyous, vivacious woman, with an open smile and an infectious laugh, but when she submitted to him, it was as if all the deep recesses of her soul poured out and she offered up to him her fears, her inhibitions, and her unwavering faith. The only photos of her smiling were the ones that showed Evan penetrating her. She always smiled when he was inside her. The contrast between the two sets of photos was always startling. It was as if his possession of her provided her what she needed to embrace the totality of her heart. He'd always been humbled by her.

Evan's fingers lightly stroked the images of his woman. He traced the contours of her high cheekbones and creamy skin. He outlined her long, flowing black hair and full lips and brushed over the lids of her dark chocolate eyes. His gaze roamed her tall, ripe body. He'd loved this album. They'd added to it regularly over the years, but it had been collecting dust for over a year since he'd last opened it.

Right about the same time he'd given up on masturbating. The pain was too much. Tonight, though, his body was making demands on him and he wasn't up to fighting it. Better to get it over with and then finish the bourbon and pass out.

Tentatively, Claire rested her hands on her belly and took in the sensations on her skin. The warm suck of the water surrounded her body and lapped gently at her breasts, which just barely peeked out from the water. She brushed her fingers along her belly, feeling the contours of her hips and navel, before sweeping gently into the springy curls at the apex of her thighs. She swirled the hair gently with one finger as anticipation curled through her. It was now or never.

Claire spread her legs and propped her feet up, one on each side of the tub, and relaxed down into the water so that it brushed her chin. She gently rested one hand on her belly and lightly stroked down across her vagina, absorbing the feel of it. The flesh was soft and a little puffy. Her outer lips pillowed around the velvet ridge of her inner folds, and she clenched instinctively. She closed her eyes and took a deep breath. She was being silly. All she needed to do was touch herself; she wasn't committing murder, dammit.

Claire took a deep breath and exhaled completely, forcing her body to relax. Gently, she dipped her finger into her folds. The flesh was soft and malleable, shaping itself to the contours of her finger. As she brushed down, she grazed her clitoris, still tightly in its hood, and she felt the shiver of excitement at the inadvertent touch. She continued down until she came to her entrance, pausing for only the barest second before plunging her finger inside.

The sensation was pleasant, as if her tongue had become conical and wrapped completely around her finger, rather than one side. She was warm and silky soft. Claire raised her hips a bit to get deeper and felt the contraction of her inner walls. Experimentally, she clenched and unclenched few times as she pressed in and out. The feelings were pleasant, but they made her long for more. For greater and deeper penetration.

She added another finger to the mix and began to flex her hips in rhythm to her pumping. The heel of her hand made luscious contact with her clitoris, slowly rising out from underneath its hood. She felt her moisture flowing and coating her fingers as she played in her pussy. Ribbons of pleasure radiated out from her core as scenes from *Finding Herself* ran through her mind. Not really knowing where to go from here, she decided to follow the choreography laid out for her in the book.

Pulling out, she began to stroke gently up and around her clitoris, exploring the folds and teasing the edges of her nub. Each teasing brush added to the sensations building inside her. She continued her exploration, enjoying the feel of her slippery flesh and stroking finger. She couldn't remember ever being touched like this. Maybe Charlie had early on, but it was so long ago it had faded into the mist of memory. She felt untouched and almost virginal in her curiosity.

Her breathing grew ragged and her nipples peaked harder as they rhythmically broke the surface of the water. In the book, Carol had been ordered to play with her nipples, but Claire didn't know if she was ready for that. Tabling that decision, she began to circle her clit with two fingers, gently rubbing along the hardened nub. The sensations, combined with the memories of the book, were creating a level of pleasure she'd never before experienced. At some point, her mind had switched from memory to fantasy, and in her mind it was now her spread out on the bed, open to the hungry gaze of her lover. She was blindfolded and could only feel as he roved her pussy with hard, firm strokes that never faltered even as she squirmed under the growing intensity.

Tension grew as Claire stroked harder, flexing her hips and driving herself harder and harder, but she still wanted more. She lost herself to the fantasy, releasing herself from her inhibitions in this one moment and reached for her nipple. She stroked and rolled her nipples at her lover's command, enjoying the streaks of fire that ran from them to her clit until he whispered in her ear, "Come for me."

Claire squeezed and tugged hard, feeling that cord stretch tight one last time before she broke, crying out as fire radiated out from her core, shivering through her. She bucked and jerked as she continued to stroke her clitoris until she finally stilled.

She brought her legs back down into the cooling water and lay for some time with her hands hugged tight around her. That had been the most intense orgasm she'd ever given herself. And yes, part of that was definitely down to touching herself properly, but a huge portion had been the fantasy. The submission to her imaginary lover. A lover who, if she was being completely honest, sounded just a bit like Evan.

~~~

As he waited for the water to warm up, Evan stripped and dropped his clothes in the hamper. His bathroom was purely serviceable, with no decoration of any kind save for the very soft, plush navy blue towels. The bathroom was white everywhere. White tiles, white walls, white tub. He supposed the blue towels and stainless steel fixtures gave it a nautical sensibility, but he really didn't care. It served his needs and that was all that mattered to him.

While he brushed his teeth, Evan considered himself in the mirror. He didn't like what he saw. He looked old. Haggard. His once jet-black hair was now graying at the temples and he sported more lines around his eyes and mouth. They weren't laugh lines either; they were the markings of pain and grief. His eyes were currently bleary and promised to be bloodshot in the morning. The rest had remained remarkably unchanged. He was tall and lean from lots of swimming, his preferred method of distraction. His muscles were still firm and he wasn't showing any of the telltale signs of softening that came with middle age. He supposed he was relatively well preserved for forty-five.

He swished and spit and still he didn't get into the shower, despite the coils of steam rising from behind the navy blue shower curtain and fogging his mirror. He simply stood there, naked as the day he was born, and stared at the shower. He didn't want to do it. He didn't want to feel anything sexual. He had learned to live with his celibacy. He'd embraced it even. Anything was better than the pain.

Blowing out a rough breath, Evan stepped under the wet spray.

The hot water pummeled his skin with searing, stinging punches. He quickly adjusted the temperature and, turning, planted himself under the warm, wet fall so that the water coated his body. The heat seeped into his muscles, loosening him up and relaxing the tension he hadn't even realized had settled between his shoulder blades. For long moments, Evan simply absorbed the moist heat into his body. He blanked out everything except the feel of the water smacking his skin and then stroking down his body.

The water flowed off his penis in wet rivulets. Tiny streamers stroked him, the damp heat reminiscent of small tongues on his flesh. Evan contemplated his dick. For the last year the only time he'd touched it had been purely functional. He barely remembered touching himself in pleasure. It was kind of like meeting up with someone you used to be really close with only to find out that you didn't really have anything in common anymore. Instead of falling back into easy camaraderie, there were long, awkward silences and uncomfortable avoidance.

He squeezed his eyes shut and tipped his head back, letting the water fall across his face. He really didn't want to do this, but after what had happened with Claire he knew it was better to get it over with. An apple a day and all that. As if to confirm the thought, his cock stirred at the image of her delicate face that formed in his mind, but there was no way he was masturbating to Claire. His brain seemed to disagree, since this time the image of her hard nipples flashed through his mind. His cock twitched and lengthened painfully.

Oh. Hell no.

Evan thought back to the album and his favorite image of Marianne, cuffed and kneeling. His cock softened. He stared at his penis in growing horror. Taking it firmly in his hand, he began to stroke along the head as he pictured Marianne in his mind. He got softer. Panic washed through his body so hard his knees almost gave out. *No, no, no, no!*

With a fierce shake of his head, he built the fantasy, so familiar and loved, of Marianne. Eventually, he hardened. He continued to work his shaft efficiently, finding the rhythm that had once been second nature. He held her image in his mind and stroked, and stroked, and stroked. It wasn't happening. He wasn't even close. It felt good, but it was more pleasant than pleasurable.

He dropped his cock and watched it bounce before settling as it softened. Damn her. Why'd she come into his store? His cock punched out into full hardness at the thought of Claire. Horror flooded Evan at his body's betrayal. *No fucking way!*

Again, Evan squeezed his eyes shut and studiously formed the image of Marianne in his mind. This time going more graphic and raw. He remembered taking her from behind, plunging into her rapidly and gripping her hips so hard he would leave behind handprints. He took the fantasy further, imagining pulling out and pressing deeply into her ass. He'd always loved fucking her that way. She'd loved it too. Pressing back into him, bucking against him as he ground into her. His cock stayed hard.

OK, I can do this.

He stayed with that image. Her round ass squeezed around his cock as he plunged in and out. The ruby pucker of her anus stretched around his cockhead. A shiver of pleasure ran down his spine as his balls tightened. It wouldn't be long now. He felt the tightening in his lower back and he went home for the kill, building the image of the thing he'd loved best during anal sex, fisting her hair as he fucked her. The utter supplication of the position never failed to bring on a scorching orgasm. Evan imagined trailing his eyes up her body, the silky skin and finely boned ridge of her spine, to where her long hair draped over her shoulders, and fisting the honey-colored locks—

What? No! Not honey, black!

The anguished thought flooded Evan's brain as his eyes snapped wide. Too late. His cock spasmed and bucked as his orgasm seized him brutally. Jet after jet shot from his body as waves of pleasure washed over him. Shaking, Evan leaned his head back under the water and let the rivulets wash across his face, all the while telling himself his eyes really just burned from the hot water.

Chapter 4

"Nice job." Bridget ross came over to congratulate Claire on leading the discussion on the club's most recent selection. Jean had been quite serious about Claire leading that second discussion and, in the weeks that followed, she'd called on Claire to lead the discussion twice more.

That first time had been excruciating for Claire; she was the perpetual shadow, not the holder of the spotlight. Claire was a member of many online groups in a variety of communities, but she was a lurker by nature, not a joiner. She liked to sit back and read or listen to discussions, but she rarely joined in unless something was so compelling that she just couldn't be quiet.

Jean, however, wouldn't be dissuaded no matter what Claire said. It was as if she'd decided to take Claire under her wing or something. She was constantly asking Claire's opinion or deliberately putting her in a position to have to join the discussion. Claire had caved in the end and she had to admit it was nice to be a part of the group rather than just on the fringes. She'd even struck up an acquaintance with Bridget, a fellow newbie.

Bridget was a chemistry professor at the local university, a fact that never failed to amuse Claire. She looked like she should be a member of the Pussycat Dolls, not teaching college freshmen about protons and electrons. She was so short at an even five feet she made Claire seem tall. Her luxurious, golden-red hair was long and curly and she kept it neatly tied up in a ponytail most days. She had clear,

green eyes like so many redheads, and a dusting of freckles on por-
celain skin, but she had the body of a pinup girl. With large, full
breasts and round hips, she made Claire feel positively boyish.

But, no matter how insecure she felt in her looks next to Bridget,
she simply couldn't be uncomfortable around her. The woman had
a vivacious and accepting quality about her that was infectious. She
made you feel better just being in her presence. She was unfailingly
friendly and polite. She was funny and warm. Claire had never felt so
accepted and welcomed before. In the three weeks since she'd joined
the club, she and Bridget had begun to talk more and more and had
even shared coffee a few times after meetings.

"Thanks. It's getting easier." Claire smiled at her. "I wish she'd
let me off the hook, though. It's almost as if she's made getting me
to speak at these meetings her personal mission."

"Oh, she has," Bridget said with a wave of her small, delicately
boned hand. "Jean is like a little momma cat. I've known her for
years. She was the president of the PTA when I was still teaching
high school chemistry, but only recently did she get me to join her
club. She took one look at you, my friend, and decided you were
going to open up."

Claire stared at Bridget, dumbfounded. "Why on earth would
she decide to do that?"

"All I know is she called me after your first meeting to get on
me about not showing up—I was supposed to be here that night,
but I had car trouble—and mentioned to me that there was a new
member who seemed afraid of her own shadow."

"What?" Claire gave an indignant snort to which Bridget just
raised her eyebrows. "Fine, I'm a little shy around a crowd of strangers. Is that some kind of crime?"

"All right now, hon, calm down." She leaned over and patted
Claire's knee where they sat on either side of the square coffee table
in the reading area. "You *are* afraid of your own shadow, but you're

gettin' better." Bridget had a slight twang from being born and raised in West Virginia that she hadn't quite lost. As a result, she had a lilting quality to her speech that tended to lull you as she spoke.

"What do you mean?" A touch of defensiveness coated Claire's words.

"Now, hon, let's not play games with each other. I like you and I don't lie to people I like. You lead the discussions quite well and you voice your opinions and musings on the stories, but you clam up the instant you have to share anything personal. It's almost as if you're okay with people picking your brain so long as it's neutral territory, but not with anyone getting to know you."

"*You're* getting to know me," Claire insisted as she sipped on her coffee. It was a new flavor, something rich and chocolaty, almost mochalike. The silky brew flowed over her taste buds and she swallowed rapturously. Evan served the best coffee. Next to the book selection, it was her favorite part of coming to Bibliophile.

Evan, now he was a whole different story. Where she'd really begun to feel welcome within the group, she felt only tolerated by the store's brooding owner. At least, brooding where she was concerned. She'd noticed he only seemed to be that way with her. With everyone else he was friendly and solicitous, and with Bridget, he was downright affectionate.

She didn't take offense at it, really; after what had happened that first night, she figured she'd managed to disgust him royally, but she liked Bibliophile too much to give it up. She was spending a lot of time here, reading and hanging out, and he was reaping the benefits of her book addiction, so she didn't feel like she was imposing. But, if she were being completely honest, she felt self-conscious when he was around. His treatment of her made her feel like there was something wrong with her since he was so nice to everyone else. He wasn't mean to her, he was scrupulously polite, but that was just it. He was relaxed and even joked with other customers, but with her he only spoke when it was absolutely necessary for him to do so. Other than that, he basically ignored her.

"Hon?" Bridget drew her attention back to their conversation. "Did you hear me?"

Claire flushed brightly. "I'm sorry, Bridget. My mind wandered. What did you say?"

"I asked you why you shy away from sharing anything remotely personal?"

Claire stared down into her coffee, wondering how to respond to Bridget. She liked her too much to lie to her, but she wasn't sure she was ready to face her rejection if she knew too much about her past. Bridget sat quietly, sipping her coffee, and just waited.

Claire set her coffee down on the table and clasped her hands in her lap. Several times she took a deep breath to start speaking. Even went so far as to open her mouth. Each time, though, nothing came out. She probably looked like a beached fish. She clenched her hands tightly in her lap and took another deep breath…

"I was raped."

"What!" Claire spluttered as her own words died on her lips.

"It happened when I was twenty-two and too trusting of the world for my own good." She gave Claire a sad, tight smile. It was the first time Claire had ever seen her look uncomfortable. "I was visiting a friend at his dorm in order to return the notes I'd borrowed. He'd warned me about coming to his dorm unescorted, but I hadn't been able to reach him and figured I'd just slip them under his door. I was on my way out and one of his floor mates came out and started talking to me. I had seen him before and thought he was cute. He invited me into his room to talk"—she put air quotes around *talk*—"and, well, he raped me." She leaned over and picked her coffee back up. Claire saw the cup tremble just a little.

"Why are you telling me this?" she asked softly. She was stunned at Bridget's revelation.

"Because," Bridget put her cup back down and faced Claire, her tone softly brisk, "you need to understand that everyone has secret shames that they hide. Things in their past that they wish didn't exist or they could redo, but those things don't have to define us. Mine doesn't and *yours* don't have to."

Claire stared at Bridget for several long moments. Her clear, green eyes were warm and just a bit sad, but she saw only sincerity in them. Claire wanted to share with Bridget, share her shame. Maybe then she could work through it, but she was also afraid. Bridget was the first person she'd felt any connection to since she was a child. And, Claire realized in that moment, Bridget's opinion mattered to her.

It wasn't often that Claire met someone she felt she could respect. Bridget had proven to be everything she said she was and Claire was almost in awe of her. She was so open and affectionate. And now, knowing how she'd been violated, that feeling of awed admiration only deepened. This, of course, meant Claire was even more intimidated by her.

This is it, Claire. Your first real test. Are you going to live or continue to die a little every day?

Claire picked her own coffee up from where she'd placed it on the table. All desire for the drink had fled; she just wanted something to do with her hands. "I—" She faltered, but determinedly straightened her shoulders, took a deep breath, and said, "I spent over fourteen years in an abusive relationship with a man I didn't love. But—" She held up a hand to stave off whatever Bridget was about to say. She'd opened her mouth, clearly intending to speak. "No, let me finish, please. You see, I was the abuser, not him."

Bridget looked confused, but she relaxed back into her chair and quirked her head expectantly. Claire paused as nausea roiled her belly. She didn't want to talk about this. Didn't want to ruin what good opinion of her Bridget might have. She'd enjoyed Bridget's company. Looked forward to it as much as the reading she did here. She wasn't ready for it to end.

She didn't really know how to explain her relationship with Charlie to Bridget. On the surface, any third party would think it was a typically abusive relationship. One where she'd been physically beaten repeatedly. The one other time she'd attempted to explain it to someone they had attempted to convince her she had battered woman syndrome because she kept insisting that it wasn't Charlie's fault.

The thing was it really wasn't Charlie's fault. He had done everything possible to get her to deal with her past when they'd met. Each and every time he'd start trying to get her to talk she'd pick a fight with him. At first, she hadn't noticed the pattern, but eventually she did. She didn't want to talk about her childhood or her family. It hurt too much and she felt overwhelmed with rage and pain. She wanted to fight; she didn't want to hurt. Hiding in the anger, she would provoke him.

She knew each and every button to push. They'd been dating for nine months when he hit her for the first time. They'd argued over whether or not she was flirting with some guy on the street. She'd been so hateful to him throughout the argument. Then, after she'd told him to fuck off, he'd slapped her. He cried afterwards and vowed he'd never touch her again. And he'd stuck to it for several years. The crazy thing was that they'd had the best conversation they'd ever had after he hit her. She'd cried and had been self-righteous about him hitting her, but she hadn't actually been mad at him at all. She'd just thought she was supposed to be mad, so she'd gone through the motions.

She'd spent every argument after that seeing how far she could push him. Would he snap? Would he hit her again? He was so good. Everything about him was so good. That was the word that summed him up: good. He didn't lie. He was courageous. Affectionate. Loving. Generous. She felt incredibly inferior next to him. She'd never been any of those things. She'd always felt dirty, less, unworthy, unlovable. She'd lied to everyone constantly, making herself out to be stronger, more dynamic. Anything other than what she really was. She'd even lied to Charlie to get him to date her.

After a while, their relationship was so bad that the arguments were relentless. Sometimes they'd literally go on all night long. He held firm, though. He didn't touch her. Claire wouldn't have been able to articulate why she needed to push him the way she did if a gun had been held to her head. It was almost a compulsion. They'd fight and she'd see the rage building inside him. See him struggle to control himself and all she wanted was to bring him down to her level. Force him to be fallible.

One day, she got her wish. The argument had been particularly vicious. He was convinced she was lying to him about being with another man. She'd never cheated on him, but she didn't do anything to make him feel comfortable with this fact. She eventually got tired of arguing and admitted that, while she hadn't cheated on him, she'd kept from him the fact that she had slept with an old friend from high school before they'd met. On the surface, that seemed trivial. The problem was that he'd asked her directly about her sexual partners and she'd lied and then maintained that lie for two years. Charlie had lost it. He'd hit her repeatedly and when she'd fallen to the floor he'd kicked her.

She'd cried and begged and pleaded for him to stop, but inside she'd felt at peace. She'd felt she was finally good enough because he wasn't so perfect anymore. She'd felt as if she could finally handle the pain raging through her, as if the tears were a release and she could finally breathe. The bruises healed quickly, and were easily forgotten, but now she had what she needed—the key to pushing him over the edge.

The sound of a book slapping the floor startled Claire out of her thoughts. Bridget sat patiently waiting, her green eyes alight with curiosity. Taking a deep breath, Claire set her coffee down and looked directly at Bridget. "Let me explain…"

Evan knelt to pick up the book he'd dropped and calm his racing heart. He moved slowly so as not to betray his presence. He'd come to the back of the store to reshelve the books customers had left out over the course of the day. He tried to keep on top of the stack so that he could close out quickly each night. He also wasn't a guy to sit around twiddling his thumbs. Mindy, his part-time helper, was off sick today and none of the morning's books were put back.

He hadn't meant to eavesdrop. Owning a bookstore, you learned to tune out most people's conversations. For whatever reason, people seemed to believe that because you were talking to someone specifically, everyone else around you didn't exist. He'd heard a lot of crazy conversations until he'd acquired the selective hearing necessary to give his customers their privacy.

Evan had been tackling the New Age section when he'd heard Bridget talking with Claire. He'd been a bit surprised that she'd confessed her rape to Claire so soon after meeting her. Evan knew about it; he'd been friends with Bridget for years now. She'd been one of his very first customers after he'd opened the store. She and Marianne had clicked when they'd met and she'd been a good friend to him in the days after Marianne's death. Evan knew that Bridget was very protective of that information. She didn't like to be perceived as a victim. The fact that she'd told Claire meant she was feeling particularly simpatico with her.

No, what had shocked Evan and had him dropping books on the floor was Claire. Evan was having a hard time absorbing what she was saying. She seemed so fragile, so timid. Believing that she had provoked repeated beatings was like asking him to believe the sky was red. It flew in the face of his expectations. It also had him wondering if she'd ever heard of impact play. Given the fact she hid every title she read from his Erotica section, he doubted highly that she did. She seemed to be completely new and naive to it all.

He'd noticed her selections the evenings she stayed to read. She was working her way through his Erotica section pretty quickly, but was focusing on light dominance and submission stories. She never bought any of the books either. She simply read them in the store and placed them back on the shelf before leaving.

The knee on which Evan was kneeling was beginning to protest his prolonged stay in that position. Shards of pain were spearing through his thighs and down his calf. Hardwood floors didn't make for comfortable kneeling. He eased himself down onto the floor, doing his best to remain silent and praying no customers would come in. He wanted to hear what Claire was saying.

She spoke in a low voice, forcing him to strain to hear her words. She was telling Bridget about the beatings she provoked from her ex-boyfriend. Her words were clipped and strained, as if she was prying each one out of some dark recess in her brain. The staccato nature of her words let Evan know this was not something she spoke of often or with ease. Finally, she quieted and the silence drew out.

Evan found himself praying that Bridget would be compassionate with her. He was aware that while she'd never been judgmental of the life he and Marianne had chosen, she also wasn't a practitioner. Her proclivities were as vanilla as they came. It was possible that what was so clear to Evan might not even occur to Bridget and, if she handled Claire incorrectly right now, Claire might never realize the truth of her situation.

The silence dragged on, stretching the air tight like a rubber band. The waiting was beginning to grate on Evan. He wanted to see what was going on, but decided against moving for fear of drawing Claire's attention. Hell, he wanted to shout at Bridget to answer already. Just as he thought he'd explode from the anticipation, he heard rustling from the back. Someone was moving around, and then Bridget finally broke the silence.

"Don't cry, hon," she said. Evan's body went rigid at her words. An insane urge to go comfort Claire swamped him. "Shh, darlin', it's clear you regret what you did to him, but I think you haven't forgiven yourself."

Evan managed to stay where he was, but he risked a quick glance around the stack. Bridget now sat on the coffee table, her back to him. She appeared to be holding Claire's hand. Claire's head was down and she was wiping frantically at her eyes. His heart clenched at the sight of her in pain. Claire began to raise her head and Evan ducked back behind the stacks.

"How can I?" Claire's normally smoky voice was liquid with tears. "I damaged him. He has never been the same man. He eventually stopped hitting me no matter what I did to him, but by the end of our relationship, he hated me. He told me so."

"He probably did hate you, hon." Bridget spoke in a soothing tone, but Evan frowned at her words. They were less than sympathetic. "You manipulated him into doing something he didn't want to do. That was abusive, you're correct, but your real mistake was in not seeking to understand why you were doing it and, if you agreed with your rationale, finding someone willing to do it to you."

Claire snorted in a derisive exhalation. "Who on earth is willing to beat a woman who isn't some kind of ax murderer?"

"You'd be surprised. You're not the only person in the world who receives a physical or psychological benefit from being beaten. The key is to find a partner who is experienced and who knows how to do it without truly harming you."

"Isn't the beating harming me by definition?"

"No, darlin', it's not. The beating is the experience you're looking for, and because of that it is a benefit to you. It's only when mistakes happen or your partner goes too far that harm happens.

Once it goes beyond the realm of what you negotiated…" Bridget exhaled roughly. "Listen, hon, I'm really not the right person to instruct you in this. I don't practice BDSM, but I've been exposed to it a little bit."

"BDSM? Are you talking about sadomasochism? I'm not into whips, chains, and blood!" Claire's voice was shrill.

"No, hon. I'm not," Bridget soothed. "There are people who get into a more extreme version of what I'm talking about, but I'm talking about beating play or something along that line. I don't recall the name. I know Evan has an Erotica section; you should see if you can find some books there. It will give you the info I don't have."

Ding. The bell over the door snapped Evan's attention away from the women. He stood as smoothly as possible and headed to the front of the store. The women's conversation faded gently as he greeted the new arrival. Bridget was right. Claire needed to understand that while what she'd done was wrong, it was wrong because Charlie was an unwilling participant. Her underlying need was one many people had. She wasn't crazy or deranged. The term Bridget had been looking for was "impact play" and Evan had just the book in mind for Claire. The problem was how to get it in her hands without giving away that he'd overheard.

Chapter 5

"You staying, hon?" Bridget asked as their reading group broke up for the evening. The group milled around them as they grabbed coffee and snacks before heading home.

"Yup," she said around a mouthful of chocolate chip cookie. She needed to watch how many of these she ate. She was beginning to put on weight. "I don't feel like going home just yet. It's too nice to be home." Claire avoided looking at Bridget as she spoke, knowing the flimsiness of her excuse showed, given that she was just going to be sitting in a bookstore rather than sitting in her house, but she didn't want to talk about it right then. Besides, Bridget already knew why she was staying at Bibliophile rather than going home.

Despite her confession about Charlie, Bridget hadn't changed her demeanor with Claire. If anything, the shared confidences seemed to have opened a door that made it possible for them to talk candidly. For the first time in her life, Claire felt able to talk unreservedly with another human being and it made her grateful for Bridget's presence in her life. That didn't mean, however, that she wanted to pluck raw nerves again and again. Especially since two major things hadn't changed and one had actually gotten worse.

The first was the fact she was still unable to purchase any of the erotica books that she read. Complicating that fact was the very real circumstance of her addiction to the genre. After that first night, she devoured the books like a starving woman confronted with food. Every new story fed a previously unknown longing inside her. She absorbed each one, taking them deep into her, and she could feel something inside her changing, growing, and becoming elastic. She hadn't yet attempted to read any of the truly hardcore books, sticking instead to sexual submission, though recently she had read a few stories with bondage and spanking.

She was comforted to realize that she wasn't the only person exploring the Erotica selections. Someone else was clearly going through the same process she was. She often found books sitting out on the coffee table waiting to be reshelved. In fact, the last two books she'd read, she'd found already out. Whoever it was, though, had harder inclinations than she did. While she was picking out only light D/s stories, this person was going for harder elements. Enter the bondage and spanking.

She'd almost put the first book back down when the story had turned to bondage. She hated to feel helpless, and the thought of allowing someone to tie her down so that she couldn't protect herself frightened her. Her body had betrayed her, though, and, as she'd come to the end of the chapter, she was once again dripping wet. A state that was becoming a near constant for her.

When she examined her reaction, what she realized was that it wasn't the bondage itself that frightened her; it was the reality of having to trust your partner with your physical safety. Trust was very hard for Claire. She didn't trust anyone but Chester. Growing up, Claire's parents had used every opportunity to humiliate and embarrass her. They weren't physically abusive in any way; more neglectful, really. Claire began taking care of herself more or less at the age of ten, doing everything short of cooking her own meals—the one thing her father demanded of her mother. What they were was emotionally abusive, and it had devastated Claire's self-confidence. She had learned very young not to trust anyone with her deeper self because the only thing they would do is use it to hurt you.

The only creature Claire trusted growing up was the family cat, Baxter. She confided her fears and dreams to Baxter, slept with Baxter curled up next to her, and loved that cat with everything she had. It was the beginning of Claire's deep love of animals. She recognized that her connection to her pets was reactionary. Animals didn't betray you and they never rejected you. It was like that with Chester. He adored her, protected her, and made her feel special with his canine affection. His devotion was a balm on her psyche. One she'd needed badly. She still didn't really trust people, though, and that was what frightened her about bondage.

Bondage required intrinsic trust—in both your physical and your emotional safety. The things a person could do to you while tied up made her shiver both in fear and anticipation. And that very dichotomy was why she'd continued to read. And why she was going to read the selection she'd found lying out tonight which combined bondage and impact play. She'd finally learned the term Bridget had sought.

She'd quickly skimmed the back before setting her other selections down on top of it to hide it. Bridget knew she was reading through the store's erotica collection, but Claire didn't really like to talk about it. She was still a bit embarrassed, mostly because it was all so new and unnerving. She was constantly surprised by how her reading was changing and shaping her desires. Or maybe *exposing* was the better word.

Each story she read was like recognizing a piece of her personal puzzle that she'd been blind to. Clearly, she found bondage erotic and exciting. You could have put a gun to her head and she'd have denied that before reading the book, though. And spanking. That one caused Claire to seriously consider counseling, given the fact that her mother had been fond of spanking Claire with a flyswatter or wooden spoon, sometimes a leather belt.

She'd been spanked so often that she'd learned to tolerate the pain and refused to cry. She wouldn't give her mother the satisfaction.

She still remembered the time Mom had broken the flyswatter trying to get a tear out of Claire. The plastic handle had just snapped. She'd hated her mother for each and every blow landed, so the idea of being sexually excited by spanking mortified Claire.

She'd decided she was sick and in need of psychiatric intervention. Claire had been so scared she'd eventually broken down and confessed her fears to Bridget over lunch at the local deli. Bridget had laughed at her, then apologized profusely when she'd realized that Claire was serious. She'd asked Claire one simple question. "Did you get excited when your mother hit you?"

Claire had been so indignant she'd almost hollered "No!" in the middle of the restaurant they were seated in. She'd managed a harsh hiss instead, but she'd been furious at the insinuation.

Bridget had just raised an eyebrow and said, "So, the two things are completely separate, then. You need to determine if you're okay with getting spanked in a sexual situation and stop conflating the two."

Claire had been speechless. There was no way it was that simple, but when she'd thought about it later, she'd realized none of her feelings had changed in regard to her mother's chosen form of discipline. She still remembered it with resentment and loathing. But when she thought about her imaginary Sir spanking her, she got wet. It had confounded her for a while, but eventually she'd realized the difference was that in her fantasy there was trust and love present. She trusted her Sir to protect her, and the spanking she would receive was about the juxtaposition of pain and pleasure.

In the stories she read, the spanking served to enhance the ultimate pleasure. Sometimes there was discipline involved in the stories where spanking was a punishment, but underlying them all was love. Her mother had been trying to hurt Claire, plain and simple. The spanking elements of BDSM were about sensory exploration and the heightening of pleasure. But either way, she wasn't ready to talk about it with Bridget.

Claire hadn't yet gotten used to the idea of being not just curious but desirous of the experiences that BDSM had to offer. She was still surprised to find that each new element she discovered touched places deep inside her. Places she hadn't known were in her. All of this new experience had translated into her fantasy life almost against her will. She masturbated often now and, after that first time, she was no longer shy about touching herself. She was even considering buying her first dildo.

Her fantasies had changed too. No longer were they rote doggy style sex with cliché partners. Now, she had elaborate fantasies of submission and bondage. She fantasized about being spanked and denied orgasm. Weirdly, she almost couldn't come until her fantasy dom gave her permission. Fantasy dom, right. Claire gave a mental snort. Evan—until Evan gave her permission. Her number one leading man was Evan. He and he alone starred in her fantasies now.

Enter fact number two that kept her returning to Bibliophile several nights a week. She had it bad for the store's gruff owner.

Normally, Claire was content to keep people at a distance. What bothered her about Evan's exaggerated civility was that it flew in the face of her very real and deepening attraction for him. With everyone but her, he was friendly and engaging. He listened to his customers with a focus that made it seem as if they were the most important thing in his world at that moment. She'd never seen him lose his cool. Well, if you didn't count that first night with her. He created an atmosphere in his store that was welcoming and warm.

What Claire enjoyed and respected about Evan was how empathetic he seemed to be. He seemed to really understand his customers and provide them with what they needed. Over the weeks she'd been coming there she'd begun to see the same faces again and again.

He had a loyal clientele, and that said a lot. As a result, she felt comfortable and secure in Bibliophile. It was becoming her favorite place to be. So much so that she'd actually fallen asleep in the store a few times while reading, much to her mortification.

Embarrassing moments and unrequited attraction aside, Claire loved to be surrounded by books and the smells of coffee and pastry. Just knowing she could get up and pick any book up off the shelf and read it without being harassed to pay and leave was sheer joy for her. The fact that Evan was gorgeous and kind added to the atmosphere. She spent her days waiting to get to the store. In some ways it was pathetic. She still had no social life other than the club and was now haunting a bookstore just to be near a man who proved with his every action and word he wanted nothing to do with her.

He never spoke to her unless he absolutely had to. When she asked a question or required information, he gave her the barest minimum required. There were no anecdotes or friendly quips for her. Every customer seemed to benefit from his humor and grace, but not her. Hell, he was downright affectionate with Bridget, and that was really saying something because Bridget tended to be friendly yet reserved with men. Claire had asked Bridget about her relationship with Evan at lunch a few days ago after Bridget had mentioned that Evan had ordered a book she'd mentioned as a surprise. Claire's curiosity had won out over her desire to hide her attraction and she'd asked Bridget about him.

Bridget had told her about meeting him and his wife. Claire had been genuinely sad to hear he was a widower. Bridget described a relationship between Evan and his wife that sounded deep and abiding, one of mutual affection and deep respect. It had made Claire's heart clench in envy. Bridget hadn't offered any more details about his wife's death other than she'd had cancer, and Claire hadn't wanted to pry, but Bridget had been very open about how she and

Marianne had become friends and, by virtue of that, she'd become friends with Evan. All she'd really been willing to say was that when she'd understood the true nature of their relationship and had seen how truly happy Marianne was, she'd realized Evan had to be a good man because you couldn't fake that kind of love.

Bridget's words had speared deep into Claire's heart. She wanted desperately to find that connection with someone. To love and be loved. To trust intrinsically that you could be yourself and not be judged or rejected. The way Bridget talked, Evan and Marianne had shared that type of bond. Claire doubted she'd ever have that with anyone, let alone Evan. She didn't think she had that level of trust inside her, but it didn't stop her heart from racing or her body from tightening and going liquid when he was near.

"Lunch tomorrow?" Bridget's voice pulled Claire out of her thoughts. "There's a new Thai restaurant that just opened next to the university and I thought we could try it out," she said over her shoulder as she gathered up her purse.

"Sure, sounds great. I love Thai." Claire smiled up at Bridget. It still surprised her that she seemed to really have a friend in her. "Do they have a patio? Maybe I'll bring Chester and we can go to the park after."

"Oh, bring him." Bridget grinned. "I must meet the mighty Chester I've heard so much about. I saw outdoor seating, so I think we'll be fine. And, if not, we'll just find somewhere else."

"Excellent." Claire beamed.

"Twelve thirty work for you?"

"Yup, I'll see you then."

"OK, be careful. You worry me when you stay here too late. The streets are still dangerous, even here."

"I'll be OK. I promise. I'm very careful."

Bridget peered at Claire for several moments, her lips pursed. "OK. But text me when you get home."

"OK…Mom." Claire laughed at Bridget's scowl. "Go on. I'll be fine and I will text you. I promise. OK?"

Bridget sighed and nodded. "OK." Turning, she headed to the exit, calling over her shoulder, "Text me!"

Claire chuckled softly. She had to admit it was nice having someone care about her safety.

Uncovering her latest find, she grabbed her coffee and sipped languorously as she opened the book to the first chapter and the world around her fell away.

Evan stepped out of the stacks to clean up and refresh the coffee and snacks after the book club meeting. Claire was in her usual place, snuggled into the leather armchair with her back to the store. It was the only chair that didn't have to be rearranged. This had become a ritual of sorts. Each Saturday after the club meeting, she'd settle in with a stack of books and studiously ignore him until he was done. Once he'd finished, she'd switch chairs so that she faced the front of the store. He got the impression she didn't like to be caught unaware.

After that first night, Claire had become a regular at Bibliophile. Evan had been concerned that his boorish behavior had driven her off, but she now spent several nights a week at the shop. Sometimes she even dozed off during her reading. Evan had become very creative in waking her up to close the store without actually speaking to her or touching her. He refused to do either, so he'd "accidentally" slam the store room door or clear his throat loudly. Usually, that was all it took. It was bad enough that she still evoked his protective tendencies and he found himself putting out the cookies he knew she liked best and switching out the coffee with decaf in the evening so she wouldn't be wired. She drank too much coffee and was way too thin. He wanted her to fill out a bit.

He couldn't define what it was about her that both pulled and repelled him simultaneously. She was attractive, there was no doubt about that, but he'd seen plenty of attractive women in his time and hadn't felt this compulsion. She didn't even fit his usual "type." He liked voluptuous women, whereas Claire would be described more as athletic, but you couldn't convince his dick of that.

Evan was beginning to feel like he'd reverted back to being an adolescent. There were nights when he'd pass behind her to get to the store room and catch a whiff of her scent, only to have to wait it out in back until he could get his erection to deflate. Other nights, she'd fall asleep and he'd catch himself standing over her fantasizing about waking her up in ways that involved his tongue, hands, and cock.

Those nights were the worst. He felt like he was betraying Marianne every time he looked at Claire. He knew it was irrational. Marianne was dead. He couldn't betray her, but it still felt that way. To make matters worse, it was getting harder and harder not to fantasize about Claire in general. She'd walk through the door and his dick would get hard. Once, she hadn't been watching where she was going and she'd bumped into him so hard she'd almost fallen down. He'd grabbed her to keep her on her feet and she'd looked up at him in startlement, those hazel eyes wide, her lips parted, and her breathing ragged so that her breasts heaved. It had taken every shred of willpower he had to fight the very real urge to press her down onto her knees, thrust his cock deep into her throat, and just fuck her mouth until he poured himself inside her.

Of course, he had only himself to blame. After he'd overheard her confession to Bridget, he'd realized how completely naive she was about BDSM and her own tendencies and had begun to leave out books he thought she should read. He'd even added to his collection to ensure she had a full range of stories to choose from. He refused to engage her directly, but he felt compelled to help her. The last thing he wanted was her getting bad information or remaining ignorant and then falling prey to someone who recognized her submissive needs but wanted only to use her. This was not a lifestyle to be idealized, and the wrong introduction could scar someone deeply. What this meant for him, though, was that he knew exactly what she was reading and what her reactions to it were, and so did his cock.

She'd read the spanking story he'd left out and he'd almost come in his pants when he'd seen her just as she'd been that first night, two seconds away from coming right there in the store. So here he was, fighting the temptation to fuck a woman he wanted nothing to do with, while at the same time shaping and guiding her sexual desires. When he put out a selection that she responded to, his errant brain catalogued that fact and then added it to his repertoire of fantasy. As if he needed help in that regard; his fantasy life was alive and well at this stage. It needed no help. His dick was fully awake too, but he'd refused to masturbate after the disaster in the shower. He'd felt so ashamed of himself that masturbating again was not an option. This confluence of circumstances of course meant he was perpetually hard, with no relief in sight.

Evan's answer to the problem was to interact with Claire as little as possible. It was out of character for him to be so aloof with a regular customer. He could tell she noticed. There were times when he caught her looking at him and saw the confusion in her face. But he just couldn't do it. He didn't trust himself where she was concerned. His temper was too short, his control too ragged. It was better for both of them if he kept his distance.

Realizing he'd been standing there staring, again, Evan proceeded to clear out the back area and leave Claire to her reading. If only he could leave her out of his brain too.

Claire watched as Evan retreated to the front of the store. As per usual, she'd pretended to ignore him as he cleared out the back area, but in truth had watched his every movement. He was male grace personified in the way he moved. She got lost in the flex and pull of his lean muscles under his customary black shirt and jeans with each lift of a chair. The grace of his fingers so long and strong where they gripped the seats as he cleared them away.

Claire bit her lip and imagined those fingers running over her body, stroking her, teasing her. Closing her eyes, she sank more deeply into the chair, allowing the fantasy to wander where it willed. Within seconds, however, she was asleep and lost in the dream…

———

"Look at me." His deep, gravelly voice was sharp with command.

Claire's eyes snapped open in answer as she obeyed his command. He stood before her, gloriously naked. Tall and lean and wonderfully sculpted, he wore his nakedness with pride. She strained to make out his features, but only the faint glow of candles lining the room provided any illumination. The rest was in darkness; she couldn't make out any detail, but the reflection off his skin caused him to glow with an otherworldly light like some demon or angel. She wasn't sure which. The flicker of the candlelight caused the shadows in the room to dance and sway, shielding his face from her and making him appear to flow with the darkness. Her inability to focus on him for any length caused her heart to race with fear, but his voice was familiar and comforting. She knew that voice. She yearned for that voice.

"What do you see?" he asked.

"I don't know," she whispered as she struggled to see him through the rippling candlelight. "I can't focus."

"Yes, you can. You're not trying." Something dangling in his hand caught her attention. She forced her eyes to focus, to peer through the swirling light and see, to no avail.

"I can't. The candles…" Claire could only plead for understanding.

"You can."

Claire struggled harder, willing her senses to break through and see what he held, and then wished she hadn't. Her indrawn breath had his focus sharpening on her. Claire couldn't fully see him, but she felt his intensity.

"Answer me, Claire." His voice was even sharper and an edge of disapproval tinged his words. That small tone made Claire's belly clench in worry. She wanted to please him desperately.

"A rope," she murmured as fear choked her.

"That's right." He stroked her cheek with gentle fingers and Claire leaned into his palm, relaxing under his tender touch.

"Tell me what you want me to do with this rope."

Claire's chest constricted. She didn't want to be tied up. She couldn't bear being helpless.

"Nothing."

"You just broke the rules, Claire." His words dripped with disappointment.

"What? How?" she cried out, shame twisting her belly.

"You just lied to me."

"No. I don't want you to tie me up. It frightens me." Panic was making her voice go shrill.

"You're lying to me."

"No!" she pleaded in desperation. "Why are you saying that?"

He moved to stand behind her before speaking. She felt his heat scalding her from head to toe. She longed to lean into him, but didn't dare move without permission. He leaned in closer and she felt the warm silk of his erection stroke along the top of her buttocks as he raised the rope and stroked her nipple with it. The rough silk of the cord abraded the bud and dragged a moan from her. Only then did Claire realize she was naked too.

"Your nipples are hard," he whispered in her ear, so close she could feel his lips move. "Your pussy is drenched." He moved the rope between her legs and rubbed along her cleft. Claire shivered in response. "If you were truly frightened, you wouldn't be aroused."

He draped the rope around her neck so that it dangled over her breasts. It was short, maybe two feet in length. He took the ends of the rope and began to stroke her nipples with them. The rope was made of some kind of white silk, but felt rough and coarse where the ends had been sealed to prevent fraying. Her nipples, already hard, stiffened even further and jutted out from her body. He pinched them, still keeping the rope in play. She moaned as white heat lanced through her. Sensation flooded her, sending every inch of her body into high alert.

"What do you want me to do with this rope?" He repeated the question as he rolled her nipples, never letting the rope drop.

Claire bit her lip as the words he wanted to hear leaped to her tongue. She couldn't. She wasn't ready.

"Answer me." He pinched harder, bringing her to the edge of pain and causing her to jerk sharply.

A tear slowly slipped down Claire's cheek as she gave him the words he'd known were inside her. She knew he'd hurt her, knew he'd use his power over her to humiliate her, but she couldn't deny the truth inside her.

"I want you to tie me up."

"Good girl." He tipped her chin up and around and gently kissed her. She inhaled his scent of clean soap and warm male deeply into her lungs before he murmured against her mouth, "Hold out your wrists, so I can bind them."

Icy fear shot through Claire. She understood what he was doing. It wasn't enough to wring the admission from her; she had to offer herself up for binding as well. Her eyes shot to his face, desperate to see him, to gain some reassurance from him before doing so, but the candlelight still danced over him, moving the shadows and giving her no ability to focus clearly.

"Claire," he admonished her.

Summoning every ounce of inner strength she had, Claire held her arms out with her wrists stacked on top of each other, closed her eyes, and waited. She felt him move around to stand in front of her and flinched as the rope wrapped around her wrists. Felt the soft push and pull as he placed the knots that would bind her. Felt a hard tug as something cold and hard whispered over her skin, and then shot her arms over her head.

Claire's eyes popped open, and she cried out as realization hit her. He'd attached her to a hook that dangled over her head. He well and truly had her at his mercy now. Panic flooded her, racing through her veins and clenching her muscles. She yanked and pulled, fighting to flee. Sweat blossomed over her skin from her futile attempts to release her hands.

"Claire! Look at me!" he demanded, but she refused. There would be no reassurance there. Two sharp smacks on her ass broke through her terror and snapped her gaze to his. Warm brown eyes broke through the flow of light and seared through her. As she relaxed, the sting in both cheeks diffused across her skin into a pleasant heat as he stroked her with a work-roughened palm.

"Trust me."

Tears ran down Claire's face as she struggled to calm her racing heart. She closed her eyes tightly and focused on the touch of his hand. He continued to stroke her ass in gentle circles that dipped lower with each orbit until finally coming to rest between her legs, where he stroked into her wetness and penetrated her with his fingers. The rough push and pull created a pulsing heat that radiated out from the center of her body.

"I can do anything I want to you now. Anything at all. Can't I?"

The tears flowed harder, but she nodded nonetheless. With his other hand he began to knead and shape her breasts, paying both equal attention. The pleasure he was causing her shocked her, given the circumstances. Her body wasn't shocked, though, and was rapidly building toward a peak of sensation.

"That's what you're really afraid of. Isn't it? What I might do to you. How I might use you?"

Claire nodded.

He leaned in and licked up her neck as he continued to plunder her folds. The warm, wet slide of his tongue followed by a quick nip along her jaw sent prickles of desire skittering across her skin.

"Or is it that you're afraid you're going to like everything I do to you, no matter what it is? No matter how depraved your mind tells you it is."

Claire's eyes snapped open as the truth of his words sank in. She was afraid, not of being tied up, but of being a party to acts her mind couldn't accept and liking it.

"I'm going to take you places you've never been, Claire, but I'll never take you somewhere you can't live with being. Trust me."

"How can I trust you when I can't even see you?" she wailed through the tears and frustration welling up inside her.

"You can see me. All you have to do is look." His tone was gentle now, coaxing even.

"I've tried," she snapped as her frustration won out.

"Try harder." She could hear the amusement in his voice, and it pissed her off.

Claire focused one last time on the shadows covering his face, willing them to fall away. Slowly, the black faded to gray, and then cleared altogether as Evan's face came into focus. The firm lines and harsh features were sharpened by desire, and his eyes were a deep, melted chocolate.

"Evan." She murmured his name as he lifted her and wrapped her legs around his waist. The blunt head of his erection nudged her entrance and she sucked in an anticipatory breath.

He shook his head and smacked her ass, setting her skin to pleasantly burning. "Sir."

"Sir," she echoed, the word a moan of longing and anticipation.

—◦◦◦—

The low moan pulled Evan out of the task of reshelving the discarded books that the day's patrons hadn't put back. Standing, he stepped out from between the stacks to see if Claire was OK. He'd noticed that she'd fallen asleep again and wondered if she was having trouble sleeping at home—or worse, if she was ill. A lance of fear speared his gut at that thought. *Stop, damn it. Just stop.*

She was indeed still asleep. The chair swallowed up her tiny frame. He could barely see the top of her head where she was burrowed down into the soft leather. Stepping softly so as not to disturb her, he stared down at her. He couldn't resist the opportunity to look at her without risk of discovery rather than having to sneak glances her way.

She lay with her head pillowed on one arm. The soft layers of her honey-brown hair spilled across her face, obscuring her eyes but framing her lush lips, which were parted softly. She was moving restlessly in her sleep. Her legs scissored against one another, creating a swishing noise from the denim of her jeans. She shifted and turned more fully, arching as another whispered groan slipped from her lips. Her nipples were hard under the cotton of her white T-shirt. Subtly, her hips began to gyrate and flex as if to meet an imaginary lover.

Evan's breath caught at the realization that she was dreaming. About sex. Desire raced through his veins and pooled heavily in his groin. Reflexively, he reached out to touch her. *Does she dream of me?*

Before the thought even fully registered, grief swamped Evan, stealing his breath and driving him back as his chest clenched hard. He grabbed onto the nearest shelf to steady himself as he tried to force air into and out of his lungs while a swarm of bittersweet memories flooded his brain.

———

Marianne, his beloved, sweet Marianne, lay splayed on the bed before him. The ruby red of the comforter contrasted starkly with the pale cream of her skin. The custom leather cuffs he'd had made for her adorned her wrists and ankles, though he'd only attached her wrists to the straps affixed to the headboard. She was so thin now and her circulation too weak for full binding. Her long, formerly lush body was now wasted and frail. Her ample breasts had reduced at least a full cup size and she was self-conscious about it, but he'd spent long, long moments attending to her nipples. Licking and loving, worshipping her so that she would know he would always love her and her body no matter what.

In this, the last days of her disease, their lovemaking had been so sporadic due to her limited strength. Evan didn't like taxing her with even gentle sex, but she was so sweet, so insistent that she needed to feel him inside her to remind her that she was still alive, that he found he couldn't resist her.

Even then, with his cock buried deep inside her, he felt her slipping away from him. Where before she would have wrapped those gorgeous legs around his waist and met him stroke for savage, pounding stroke, laughing joyously as he claimed her, now she could only lie, a willing recipient for his loving possession.

He took her gently, resting his weight on his forearms so that the full length of their bodies touched but he wasn't crushing her. With his eyes closed, he savored the welcoming embrace of her core as she clung wetly to his cock. He committed to memory the soft rasp of her pebbled nipples against his chest as he moved against her. Imprinted the scent of her skin, ginger and honey, into his brain so that he'd never forget. He'd known, in the deepest recesses of his heart, it would be the last time he'd make love to his woman.

When she came, arching under him and whispering rather than screaming his name in his ear, he'd joined her. With each wave of pleasure he'd spilled his hopes and dreams and grief and pain over their aborted life into her body until finally he'd collapsed beside her with tears he hadn't even known he'd been shedding running down his cheeks.

She'd fallen into an exhausted sleep almost at once, and he'd unstrapped her and pulled her into his arms before finally falling into a fitful slumber. Sometime later, she'd become restless and he'd woken and soothed her, stroking her back. She'd rested a skeletal hand on his cheek, exerting just enough pressure to get him to look at her.

"I love you, baby," she whispered, her deep brown eyes awash with unshed tears.

"I love you too, doll face." He turned his lips into her palm and pressed a kiss to the center.

"Dream of me—after. Every once in a while, dream of me, so I can come and check on you."

"Always, love. I'll dream of you always." He'd settled her more comfortably in his arms and soothed her back to sleep.

When he'd woken, she'd been gone. She'd died in his arms with a peaceful smile on her face.

~~~

Evan lurched into the store room and collapsed on top of a stack of boxes, struggling to breathe through the grief choking him. He couldn't do this. Couldn't let himself want Claire. Marianne was too close, too full in his heart, and he'd stopped wanting anyone but her once they'd met. He felt as if he were betraying her, and it made him sick. They'd never invited anyone else into their bed. He hadn't wanted to. It had been just the two of them and it had been enough. But she'd died, and he missed her so much that it hurt.

He didn't want to want Claire, and the fact he did—he wouldn't lie to himself, he wanted her—was more than he could handle right now. Ruthlessly clamping down on his emotions, Evan took a deep, ragged breath and made his way to the small bathroom in the back of the store room to splash cold water on his face. When he was satisfied that he looked presentable, he returned to the selling floor only to find Claire gone and the store completely empty.

Chapter 6

"YOU LOOK AMAZING, CLAIRE." The warmth in Marcus's voice wrapped around her. She'd missed him so much. She hadn't even realized it until she'd heard his voice over the phone. It had taken every ounce of courage she could muster to dial his number, but she'd done it. And now here they were, seated across from each other sharing a meal on the patio at Luna Bella, a popular Italian trattoria.

Situated in the heart of the arts district, Luna Bella was an excellent restaurant with a unique blend of open architecture and privacy. It faced the local art house theatre, and was one of Claire's favorite places to eat. She often took in a matinee, and then popped over for a cannoli and espresso before heading home. The sweet confection and strong coffee were the perfect ending to an afternoon of cinema.

From experience, Claire knew it would not be crowded on Sunday with so many people preparing for the work week, so she and Marcus would have plenty of privacy. The weather was warm and the night clear, making it the perfect backdrop for their reunion, so Claire had asked for a patio seat.

When choosing the location for this reunion, Claire had wanted to be in a familiar setting, but she had also picked this restaurant for its proximity to her house, which meant she could walk home if the evening went badly. She'd learned a long time ago not to rely on anyone for transportation when the outcome of the evening was dicey, and this evening's outcome was definitely up in the air. The last time she'd seen her brother, they'd parted on vicious, ugly words that she'd regretted almost instantly, but her pride had kept her from taking them back. The result had been a ten-year separation from her brother, who had once been her closest friend.

Marcus had disapproved of her relationship with Charlie and he'd made no secret about it. Of course, he'd blamed Charlie for the dysfunction, absolutely refusing to entertain the notion that Claire was responsible. Instead, he'd told her she needed counseling for her delusions. Rather than continue to fight him, she'd made horrid accusations, claiming that he was jealous of her relationship, and had even insinuated he had an unnatural connection to her.

He'd slapped her. Hard. Splitting her lip and sending her reeling. She'd fallen into the coffee table and damn near cracked her head open as she'd gone toes over head before landing in a disheveled heap. Looking up at him with blood streaming down her chin and neck, she'd laughed and asked, "Now do you believe me?"

Marcus had stared at her, his face deathly pale with eyes dilated from shock for long moments before saying, "You need help," in a voice thick with tears. He'd pivoted on his heels and stormed out. It was the last time she'd seen or spoken to him, but that night had haunted her for years until, like so many of her crimes, it had blurred into the tapestry that was her life and she'd forgotten it.

Or at least, that's what she'd thought. But, like so many of her preconceived notions, she'd found out she was wrong. She'd dreamed of him. Dreamed that he was looking for her. Relived those last moments with him, but this time in the dream she ran after him, calling out for him to come back. She'd drifted back to consciousness with the conviction that she needed to call Marcus thrumming through her.

It had taken a full week before she was able to let the call go through and not hang up the moment she heard it ring. Much to her surprise, rather than hang up on her, Marcus had been ecstatic to hear from her. They'd spent hours talking and catching up. She'd even gotten to speak with his wife and young daughter. A truly bittersweet moment, because it highlighted how much of his life she'd missed. They'd talked for hours that first call. She'd apologized, and he'd been gracious. He'd told her that he still didn't understand the choices she'd made, but he was happy that she'd taken control of her life. He'd been the one to suggest they have dinner, but she'd accepted without hesitation.

She'd agonized over her appearance. She wanted to look her best. Wanted her brother to approve. She probably shouldn't care, but she did. She felt as if she was being reborn. Tonight she met her brother on new ground as a new person. She was scared to death but hoped it didn't show. She'd left her hair loose and put on a simple wrap dress in black knit. Light makeup, a single strand of pearls, and black sandals completed the outfit. She felt elegant and armored.

Marcus had made a special effort as well, donning a sport coat and button-down with jeans. Remembering his hatred of all things dressy, this definitely represented a special effort, and her heart squeezed at the gesture. The years had been good to him. His light brown hair was only slightly dusted with gray and his eyes, hazel just like hers, remained unlined. The most significant change was in his presence. Marcus had always had a lazy quality about him, one that made it easy to overlook him, but now he radiated a confident grace that made Claire do a double take when she first saw him. Rather than blending into the crowd as he'd always done, Claire had noticed him immediately. It was in the set of his shoulders and the lift of his head. No longer did he slouch or fold in on himself. Claire only hoped he saw some similar changes in her.

"Thanks, so do you." She smiled at him. "Marcus, I—"

Claire broke off as she caught sight of their waiter wending his way through the linen-covered tables as he brought out their dinner. With an efficiency born of obvious experience, he deposited their meal of lasagna and salad served family style, and left them to eat. Claire waited as Marcus served them both before again beginning to speak.

"Marcus…"

"Claire, wait," Marcus interrupted her. "I think I know what you're going to say, and let's just leave it where it belongs. OK?" He reached out and covered her hand with a warm palm. "We said all that needs to be said about the past. You're my sister. I love you and I've missed you." He grinned widely, his hazel eyes shining, before leaning closer and squeezing her hand. "That's what is most important. Let's just start over from here."

Tears flooded her eyes unbidden. It felt like a wall had just crashed down inside her and emotion was flooding through her. A happy sob escaped her, and she brought his hand to her lips, kissing the palm before placing it on her cheek. For several seconds she just held him to her, absorbing the connection before laughing out loud.

"You always did know how to make me cry."

Marcus chuckled. "At least this time I didn't cut off a hunk of your hair to do it."

Claire's joyous laughter, not just at his words, but at reclaiming such a large part of her life, floated out into the evening.

⟶⟵

Bright laughter caught Evan's attention as he stepped out of the Silver Theatre. He'd just taken in the latest installment of their annual Hitchcock festival. *Vertigo* with Jimmy Stewart was one of his favorites and, since it was Sunday, the store closed early, giving him the evening to do something fun. He might own a bookstore, but he was a film buff. He generally came to the theatre on Sunday after the store closed. They catered to classic movies with the occasional indie flick thrown in, and that suited him just fine. He didn't enjoy the crowds that generally accompanied the blockbusters.

Another trill of laughter sounded. It pulled at Evan. The joy infused in that laugh was not often heard. There were silly laughs, guffaws, belly laughs, and sarcastic laughs, but this laugh radiated happiness. Evan had laughed like that at one time, but it had been a long time since he'd felt joy that deep.

Since Marianne's death, Evan had become a connoisseur of laughter. He'd learned to recognize the nuances and shape of it. At first, it had been in reaction to the anger he felt every time someone laughed. Marianne was dead and it seemed like the world should be grieving her loss with him. He'd resented other people's happiness. Eventually, he'd come to grips with the fact that life moved on and he must too, but by then it had become a habit to catalogue the laughter he saw in the world around him. Almost as if by doing so, he was storing it up to one day be able to laugh again.

He scanned the few patrons seated on the patio at Luna Bella, searching for the source of such joy, and, like iron to a magnet, locked in on Claire and the man she was with just as she kissed his palm and cradled his hand against her face. She appeared almost transcendent in her joy. The smile on her face transformed her from attractive to resplendent, and the peace she radiated at the man's touch was almost physical. Evan had never seen her so open and relaxed.

Rage, red and searing, burned through Evan so quickly it stole his breath. Evan was halfway across the street, prepared to rip the man's hands from Claire, before sanity reasserted itself and he retreated back to the entrance of the theatre. Chest heaving, Evan struggled to regain his composure. This was exactly why he stayed away from her. He wasn't himself around her. All control flew out the window and he behaved like a Neanderthal. She was nothing to him. A customer, nothing more. She could date whoever she wanted. He didn't give a fuck. The thought barely made it through his brain before his inner bullshit meter asserted itself.

You've never been a liar, Evan. Don't start now.

Taking a deep breath, Evan sought to calm his racing heart. He gritted his teeth and clenched every muscle in his body before slowly relaxing one muscle at a time. When he was able to unclench his fists, he forced himself to admit that he did care. He'd been making a point of guiding her through her explorations of BDSM for the sole purpose of preparing her for her first experiences in it. He had a vested interest in who she dated. If her initiation went poorly, she could be harmed both physically and mentally. After what he'd heard her tell Bridget, she might never recover if that were to happen.

She wasn't ready yet. She still selected only light stories even though she devoured the ones he left out for her. He'd know she was ready the day she voluntarily picked out a story that involved more than being ordered around in the bedroom. Until then, she had no business getting herself involved with a man. Period. What relaxation he'd been able to achieve flew out the window as the image of Claire on her knees in front of the stranger seared its way into his brain. He had to get the fuck out of there.

Clamping down ruthlessly once more on the urge to go over there, Evan stalked away, determined to get home and forget about her.

Forgetting about her was proving easier said than done. Since he'd walked through the door he'd made himself a sandwich, taken a shower, done what few dishes he had, and had tried and failed to read the newspaper, all to no avail. The image of Claire with that man's hand on her cheek was burned into his brain like a brand. Each time it popped back into his head, his teeth clenched so hard his jaw ached. To make matters worse, his overactive imagination wasn't letting it stop there. No, every time he'd think he'd gotten his unruly thoughts in order, he'd get taught that he was wrong. In the shower, he'd been thinking about everything other than Claire. The chores that needed doing at Bibliophile, the paperwork he needed to finish, the fact he needed to submit his tax return…*Bam!* His brain locked on *submit*, and there she was, naked, on her knees with that same adoring look he'd seen in the restaurant.

Having your dick punch out into an erection at the same time your chest squeezes so tight you can't breathe is a recipe for disaster. He'd had to sit down on the edge of the tub until he could collect himself. It had been like that ever since he'd gotten home. An errant thought leading to a graphic image of Claire in submission. To the point where he was so on edge his skin felt brittle and strained under the rage he was struggling to hold in. The tension in his body was so profound the air around him felt thick and heavy.

If he didn't collect himself soon, he was going to have a fucking heart attack. With a mental shake, Evan grabbed the fifth of Evan Williams off the sideboard and poured himself a hefty dose of the amber liquid. Walking to his window, he stared out over the quiet street and did his best to find some perspective.

He was being unreasonable and he knew it. She was a grown woman, and free to make her own choices. But dammit, she was naive. She didn't understand the risks involved. If she wasn't careful, she might pick a man who was willing to exploit her. Use her as the punching bag she'd been so intent on being to her ex. She didn't realize how lucky she had been that he *didn't* want to use her that way. There were men who would exploit that need in Claire so badly she would be torn down, shredded, and left for dead inside before she even knew what happened.

The thought of Claire broken and helpless brought on another surge of rage so strong his hand shook as he took another deep swig of bourbon. He felt responsible for her. He was deliberately opening her mind up to experiences she might or might not be ready for, and now he was confronted with the very real possibility that she might jump in before she truly knew what she was doing. Everything in him rebelled at the notion of Claire being hurt through ignorance. But what could he do? He was doing everything he could do already.

Downing the rest of the bourbon in his glass in deep, hard swallows, Evan poured himself another and leaned against the sill of his window, doing his best to draw some peace from the serenity of the evening outside. The street below was lit with streetlights that had been designed to look like those old-fashioned gas lanterns. These were alternated with planters full of colorful flowers and greenery that gave the street a feeling of vibrancy·and life. He'd chosen this location for his store because it was exactly the kind of street that invited an easy stroll to just take in the atmosphere. He'd been convinced he'd get a lot of spontaneous foot traffic, and he'd been right.

Whenever he was out of sorts, he'd always been able to just look out his window and relax. He was a people watcher. He enjoyed imagining what the people he saw on the street might be about. It reminded him that life went on even if he felt like his had stalled out. There were only a few people out tonight, typical of a Sunday evening. A young woman of about twenty was jogging along the opposite side of the street. Her long, blond ponytail swung in time with her steps. An older man in a worn fedora and a muddy brown cardigan walked a small, white Pomeranian that was making a point of lifting its leg on every lamppost. A couple strolled leisurely along at the end of the street, headed in his direction. The man's arm was wrapped around his lady's shoulders and hers around his waist. Their body language was intimate and affectionate, and a pang of envy shot through him at their obvious closeness.

He missed that. Missed having someone you cared for in your life. Missed the intimate touches and body closeness that came from being with someone you loved, but what could he do? His love had died and he couldn't imagine finding that again.

Evan straightened and downed the last of the bourbon. It was time to go to bed. At least if he was asleep he wouldn't be thinking about Claire. As he turned, the tinkle of laughter drifted up to him and he went rigid as every hair on his body stood at attention. He knew that laugh.

Evan whirled around and leaned into the window to get a better look at the couple. They were between lights and in shadow, thwarting his effort. As they progressed toward the next pool of light their features slowly resolved. It was Claire and her mystery man, and she was smiling up at him with what could only be called adoration shining out of her face. They were headed in the direction of her town house. She was taking him home.

That realization sunk into the marrow of his bones and chilled him to the core. With a roar, Evan spun and flung his glass across the room before stomping into the bedroom and slamming the door. The tinkle of splintering glass was the only sound remaining in the empty room.

Chapter 7

SHE GLOWED. EVAN STOOD in the doorway of the store room and watched as Claire led the group's discussion of their latest selection. She was animated and vibrant and radiated a confidence he'd never seen in her before. Her eyes sparkled, and her shoulders were back and firm rather than slightly hunched. She was laughing and engaging the group. She was transformed.

Scowling, Evan headed back to the front to get a head start on the evening paperwork. She was fucking him. That was the only possible explanation. Women always glowed during the honeymoon stage of a relationship. He was probably telling her everything she wanted to hear.

He hadn't thought his mood could get any blacker. Over the last week, he'd had plenty of time to stew over the idea of Claire and her mystery man. She hadn't even come in during the week like she usually did. Just like a woman. Get a man and give up everything around them. This was exactly what he'd been worried about.

Claire was at a very dangerous phase in her exposure to BDSM. She was open and curious, with no real guidance. She needed to be handled with care and patience, to be brought slowly along. Her limits explored and gently pushed. The wrong person could get his hands on her—literally—and wreck everything Evan was trying to do.

That thought stopped him up short. What exactly was he trying to do? He wasn't trying to get into anything physical with her. He just hadn't wanted her to think her desires represented some kind of sickness. He'd wanted her to see that she wasn't alone and there were avenues for her to channel her needs productively. But, given her taste for impact play, she needed to be very careful. If it were him, he'd start with spanking, maybe progress to light flogging, before getting into anything harder. See how she responded. See if what she'd subconsciously been trying to coerce her boyfriend to do was a true need, and then channel it.

The mere thought of his hands on Claire, her round little ass turning pink, had his body raging. She had a luscious ass. Full and round. He couldn't help but notice it every time she came in, something that set his teeth on edge. But then, what didn't set his teeth on edge about the damnable woman? She was a constant source of frustration for him.

Tonight had been the absolute worst. She'd come in and he'd done a double take. He'd literally had to take a moment and figure out who this gorgeous, radiant creature that had just walked through his door was. She vibrated with a joy he hadn't ever seen in her. She'd smiled at him as soon as she'd seen him, and raised her hand in greeting, calling out a hello to him. A first. He hadn't answered, and had frowned at her when he'd realized it was Claire. Her smile had wavered a bit, but she'd visibly steeled herself, nodded at him, and gone to the back.

He hadn't meant to be rude, but he'd been stunned into speechlessness. She was wearing a form-fitting pencil skirt that hugged her ass and accentuated her waist. She'd paired it with a tailored, ruby blouse that showed off her slimness while highlighting her pert breasts. The color did amazing things for her skin too, bringing out a light pink flush that made her appear almost luminescent. Her hair was loose and she'd done something to it so that it framed her face and highlighted the delicateness of her features. The knee boots she wore gave her the impression of height, and the stiletto heels added a hint of sexy that she didn't normally convey. She looked fucking delicious. His mouth had literally watered. So had his cock. Thank God he always wore black or else a definite wet spot would have shown through his jeans.

And this was exactly why he stayed away from her. He was standing in the middle of his store, his dick hard as a rock, dripping and fighting the temptation to bend her over and spank her little ass until it burned. He expected better of himself. He'd never been this ruled by his temptations with Marianne. Evan's heart thunked, and his cock deflated. He was an ass. What was he thinking? He could never replace Marianne.

With a heavy sigh, Evan sat at the register and began running the day's sales reports. He was letting himself get caught up in something he had no business being involved in. He could never give Claire what she needed. She needed someone who could commit fully to her and be there for her emotionally. He had given his heart away and then buried it. She'd obviously found someone who made her happy. He needed to just let it all go.

"Ooof." Claire stumbled and latched on to Evan's arm as she tried to stay upright. She'd been reading the back cover of her latest erotica selection and hadn't been paying attention to where she was walking as she headed back to the seating area to read. The movement brought her into almost full body contact with him. He grabbed her as she stumbled and his arm wrapped around her waist, holding her against him. Her body reacted immediately to his nearness. Her breathing sped up and her nipples went instantly erect. Deep inside, she tingled and went damp.

He, on the other hand, seemed offended. His powerful body was rigid, the scowl on his face harsh and menacing. Those deep chocolate eyes that she fantasized about blazed with anger, and his lips were a cruel slash. She quickly pulled away from him and stepped back.

"Sorry about that." Claire took a deep breath and smiled up at him. She was determined not to let him intimidate her any longer. He might find her disgusting, but dammit, she was a paying customer and she had as much right as anyone else to be in the store. Her feelings about him were irrelevant. She was a grown woman and would deal with her crush privately. She'd get over it eventually. No longer was she going to hide and shrink.

After her dinner with Marcus, it was as if a door inside her opened. She'd never felt more in control of her own life. Reconnecting with Marcus had been that first step on the road to getting both closure with her past and to traversing the path to her future. The last week had been a whirlwind of visits with him and his family. She'd spent several evenings at their house, meeting his wife and getting to know her niece. She'd even signed up for a class in the Israeli martial art, Krav Maga. Claire had always wanted to be able to defend herself, but had been too self-conscious to do anything about it.

She might need physical pain at some level, but that didn't mean she wanted to be a victim. She'd been doing a lot of soul searching and had come to the realization that she wanted to experience what BDSM had to offer. She just wasn't sure how to go about it. The trust needed to ensure you didn't end up someone's victim was deep and she was frightened of choosing the wrong person.

The irony was that the person she felt would suit seemed offended by her very presence. Evan's kindness and generosity was apparent. He seemed deeply intuitive and was highly regarded. If Bridget trusted him, then he must be trustworthy. Bridget was nothing if not reserved and skeptical with men as a result of her rape. She trusted very few, and she had only glowing things to say about Evan. It was clearly Claire that he had a problem with. But to say she didn't want Evan to be her first would have been a lie. He was the number one star in her fantasies now. He was her Sir in her head if not in the flesh, and she found herself hoping each time she saw him to be able to make him smile rather than scowl at her, to engage him in conversation and get to know him, but so far he'd only gotten more distant.

"Sorry, I wasn't watching where I was going." Her smile turned sheepish.

"Yeah, I know," he growled at her.

Taken aback by his abruptness, she stammered, "Um…Well…OK." She started to head back to the seating area. Clearly, she wasn't going to get different results tonight.

"That was careless." He actually stepped closer and loomed over her. He was so close she could smell his scent. "You should know better than to be so careless."

Claire absolutely hated when big men used their size to intimidate her. She knew she was small; they didn't have to exploit it. She stepped back, only to come up hard against the shelves behind her. Evan stepped closer and towered over her with his hands fisted on his hips.

"What if you'd tripped and fallen? You could have hurt yourself. Especially wearing those ridiculous boots. They're just an accident waiting to happen."

"Excuse me." Claire frowned up at him. She could almost feel his anger. The muscles in his neck were tense and stood out in stark relief. His eyebrows were drawn so tightly together she wondered if they'd fuse in place.

"You're overreacting just a bit, don't you think?"

"Overreacting? I don't think so. If you hurt yourself in this store, I'm liable."

"Evan—"

"No." He cut her off. His expression was as stony as his tone.

"I'm beginning to wonder if you need a keeper. You come in here and fall asleep. You walk home by yourself after dark without any thought for the danger, and now you're not even watching where you're going. Are you stupid?"

All color drained from Claire's face at his words. Shame and humiliation warred with righteous anger. How dare he chastise her this way! How dare he insult her! The world went black then red as Claire found her voice.

"Who the *hell* do you think you are?" She poked her finger into his chest. It was rigid with tension and her finger hurt, but she didn't care. She poked him again, harder. "You have *no* right to speak to me this way. You know absolutely *nothing* about me or why I do anything I do. I think I know why you treat me like a pariah when you seem to be able to be so nice and kind to all of your other customers, but I will not stand here and be insulted by you.

"*Not* that it is any of your damn business, but I live just a few blocks away. I am extremely careful and I even signed up to learn a martial art. Yes, I take a risk, but I refuse to live my life a prisoner. I have no one in my life to accompany me here, so I either come by myself or I don't come at all." Claire was shouting at him now. She was trying to stay calm, but all of her patience had flown out the window. "But," she continued through gritted teeth, "since I apparently disgust you so badly, you won't have to worry about that anymore." She set the books she'd been carrying down on the shelf and pushed at his chest with both hands. "Now get the hell out of my way."

He refused to move, seemingly rooted in place. Instead, it was Claire who backtracked. Snatching up her tote, she rounded the stacks, and then stormed toward the door.

"Claire!" Evan called from behind her. She heard him moving quickly toward her and spun around, holding up a hand.

"Don't you come near me." Claire's breathing was ragged as rage coursed through her. "I don't want to hear anything more you have to say. You've said quite enough."

Spinning on her heel, she snatched open the door and walked home as fast as her "ridiculous" high heels allowed.

Chapter 8

SHE WASN'T COMING BACK. It had been two weeks and she hadn't shown up. Not once. Jean wasn't speaking to him and Bridget had given him the evil eye for a whole week before she'd finally relented and given him a piece of her mind. She'd heard all about how he'd been out of line, rude, obnoxious, and mean, and how dare he treat "poor Claire" that way!

Poor Claire, my ass.

Evan rubbed the now faded bruise on his chest. She'd managed to poke him hard and deep enough that he'd had a bruise just under his right pec for a week. He smiled at the memory. She'd stood up to him, no doubt about it. She'd been beautiful in her righteous anger. The light flush on her cheeks and that gleam in her eye…She'd been magnificent. His smile faded as he recalled the cause of all of her newfound confidence—her mystery man. No doubt she was spending her time with him. Evan scowled at the thought.

He'd been an ass. He'd had no right to say the things he did to her and he knew it, but how could he apologize if she didn't come back into the store? He'd meant what he'd said, though. She *was* being careless. Falling asleep in the store. Come on. She obviously wasn't taking care of herself. She needed a damn keeper. She needed to show the hell up so he could make sure she was OK.

He couldn't stop thinking about the danger he'd inadvertently placed her in. There was a reason people said that a little knowledge was a dangerous thing. What if this man she was with was as inexperienced as she was and did something that hurt her? Or, worse, what if he was experienced and deliberately set out to hurt her?

She was ripe for the picking at this stage. Her mind was fertile and open, just waiting for someone to come along and till the ground he'd made sure was ploughed and ripe for planting. *Dammit!*

"What's got you looking so foul?" Bridget plopped her books down on the counter and raised a perfectly arched eyebrow.

"Nothing." Evan picked up her books and began stacking them in order of size rather than looking at her.

"Doesn't look like nothing." She leaned against the counter. "In fact, it looks very much like something."

"Bridget, stop poking that lovely little nose where it doesn't belong." He gave her a hard look in the hopes of getting her to back down.

"Compliments will get you everywhere, my boy, but they won't back me off"—she waved a hand in his direction—"so quit trying to scowl at me. It's never worked before, it won't work now."

Evan smiled at her despite himself. He'd always liked Bridget, and he'd felt honored when he'd realized that she actually trusted him enough to relax around him. He took that responsibility seriously and had always done his best to respect that gift. Right now, though, he really wished she'd just mind her business.

"Evan"—she reached out and placed her hand over his where it lay on her stack of purchases—"you're going to have to make this right. This was her favorite place to be, and you ran her out of here. What is going on with you and her anyway?"

Evan snatched his hand out from under hers and stood up so fast the stool pushed back. "Nothing. Absolutely nothing is going on with us." He grabbed up a bag and began shoving her books inside. "What makes you say something like that anyway?"

"Oh, I don't know. Maybe the fact that you get all snarly and scowly when she's mentioned. You blew up at her for no reason.

Something you've never done, not even with Marianne. And now, the mention of her name has you acting all defensive."

Evan came around the counter and handed Bridget her purchases. Placing a firm hand on her lower back, he unceremoniously guided her toward the exit. Opening it with one hand, he all but pushed Bridget out the door.

"Love you, Bridget, but I'm closed."

Locking the door behind her, Evan flipped the sign to Closed and headed back to the register to close out.

Bridget meant well, but she was treading on dangerous water. And of course, he'd never blown up at Marianne; she'd had him to look after her. Claire, on the other hand, didn't have anyone. Scratch that, *had* no one. She was with mystery man now.

Dropping the money he'd been counting, Evan sighed deep and hard. He was going to have to find a way to get her back in the store so he could check up on her. If anything happened to her, he'd be responsible, and he didn't want that on his head.

Bridget sat behind the wheel of her Mustang and watched Evan through the bay window. That man was lying to himself or her name wasn't Bridget Ross. She'd never seen him so disturbed. He was prickly and distracted and downright defensive at the mere mention of Claire's name. She'd wondered if the day would ever come that he'd wake up and remember he was alive.

She'd loved Marianne dearly, but Mari was dead and Evan was alive. He could do much worse than Claire. Oh, she'd heard all about how Evan had dressed Claire down like a child. She'd also heard how Claire had stood right up to him and given him a piece of her mind. She'd been proud of her new friend. Claire needed more self-defining moments. She also needed Evan to wake up and realize he wanted her. Claire wasn't under any self-delusions on her end. She knew she had it bad for Evan, and staying away was killing her.

Again, Bridget had to give her friend props for sticking to her guns. But she had a feeling there was more going on here than was apparent. Something had triggered Evan's outburst. That was very out of character for him.

Claire, for her part, had blossomed. She'd finally reconnected with her brother…Bridget's gasp was audible as pieces of the puzzle fell into place. Evan routinely went to the Silver Theatre, Claire and Marcus had gone to Luna Bella—had he seen them?

Bridget grinned as she started the Mustang and pulled out into traffic. Oh yes, Evan was definitely waking up.

Claire's finger hovered over the Delete button on the screen of her phone. Twice now she'd listened to the message, and twice she'd told herself to delete it. Her finger descended, pressing lightly on the screen, and Evan's voice filled the loft.

"Claire. This is Evan from Bibliophile. I'm calling to inform you that you are the winner of the free book for the Sexy Summer Reads contest. All of the book club members were automatically entered and you're the winner. Please stop by the store to claim your free book at your convenience. Thank you."

She could feel herself wavering. Her damn hands were even shaking just from the sound of his voice. Her name in his smoky timbre sent little shivers along her spine. Staying away from Bibliophile had been one of the hardest things she'd had to do, but there was no way she was going to stay there and let him talk down to her like that. Regardless of what he might think of her, she wasn't an idiot, and she just couldn't stand back and take his disgust and disdain any longer. She was claiming her life for better or worse, and that included not allowing herself to be talked down to.

A sharp pain jabbed into Claire's palm. She was gripping the phone so tightly her knuckles were white. Inhaling deeply, Claire forced herself to relax. She wasn't angry so much as hurt. The sad reality was that she was lost on him. Despite her best efforts, she just couldn't get him out of her head. He was in her dreams, her fantasies, her thoughts. He had become a near-constant drumbeat in her mind.

She wanted badly to return to the store, as much for the environment and people she'd come to enjoy. Jean's call this morning had been hilarious in its absurdity.

"Claire. This is completely unacceptable." Jean's voice had been shrill enough to cause Claire to hold the phone away from her ear. "You have to come back. I'd finally broken you, after all. I'm kidding, of course, but only a little bit." She laughed, a long, horsey laugh, but Claire smiled nonetheless. Jean was good people.

"Jean…" She tried to interrupt the deluge that Jean was hurling her way. No such luck. Eventually, Jean's voice faded into a shrill *whah, whah, whah* like Charlie Brown's teacher.

"OK?" Jean's narrative suddenly took shape again on the question.

Claire's pulse jumped. She had no idea what Jean had asked her. With a sharp, mental shake she just winged it.

"Jean, look. I really enjoy the club, but I'm just not sure right now if I'll be back."

At Jean's deep inhale, Claire rushed forward to stave off another flood. "Now, I'm not saying no. I'm saying let me think on it, OK?"

"Well…" Jean drew the word out as if she were looking for a weakness in Claire's defenses. "I guess, but I'm not happy about this not one bit. Why, Evan got an earful from me, he did. I don't know what's gotten into that man, he never acts like this. It's so out of character. I've just never seen him this way."

"What do you mean?" Claire cringed even as the words left her mouth. She didn't want to know. Really, she didn't.

"I mean he's stomping around his store like a bear with a sore paw. I've never seen him act so grumpy. Not even when Marianne was sick. You'd think he'd lost a fight or something."

Claire had no idea what to make of that, and her silence had apparently translated to Jean as permission to launch into another monologue on how no one was cooperating with her and if everyone would just get on board with her, things would resolve themselves.

Finally, Jean blew herself out, and Claire graciously ended the call with promises to think hard about coming back to Bibliophile. Sitting there now, though, Claire felt no more certain than she did before. The last thing she needed right now was an even more surly Evan making her feel stupid. She was only just starting to feel like a human being again.

Nope, no thank you. With a decisive nod, Claire called up the message on her phone and deleted it.

The bell chimed as Claire entered Bibliophile. She was a goddamned fool, but the instant she'd deleted Evan's message she'd scrambled and cursed herself as she tried to get it back. Who came up with the brilliant notion of not allowing for undeleting voice mail? Finally, she'd thrown the phone into the couch and just plopped down, her face in her hands. She was ridiculous. He didn't want her, and she was mooning over him like some kind of lovesick teenager.

A long walk with Chester and some sushi had done nothing to make her feel any better, and she'd had to come to the hard realization she was fooling herself. She was going back. He'd opened the door, whether he'd been forced to or not, and she was going to walk through it.

Now, though, standing back inside the store once again, feeling the ambiance and aromas sink into her bones, she felt both as if she'd returned home and she was about to go on trial. It really was ridiculous. She was a grown woman, not a child, and this was a bookstore of which he was the proprietor. Nothing more.

Claire snorted mentally. *Right.* She wanted Evan like she wanted to breathe, and was silly enough to just hang around him and torture herself in doing so. Even still, she wasn't willing to fully concede. She'd made sure to come fairly close to closing, giving herself just enough time to browse a bit, pick out her book, and head home. Truthfully, she already knew which book she was taking home, and she wasn't going to let embarrassment stop her, but she figured she'd take some time and browse for some other selections while she was there.

A quick glance around seemed to indicate that she was alone. The store was deserted; not even Evan was around. She refused to dwell on her simultaneous disappointment and relief at that realization. Determined to get on with things, Claire set off down the aisles, a woman with a purpose. Her shoulders were square and her head was high. As she got closer to her destination, she glanced furtively around, only to laugh out loud at her silliness and take a deep breath. It was buying a book, not drugs.

A quick scan of the shelves showed that Evan had added yet again to his erotica collection, but she wasn't interested in new selections. She was interested in the one book she'd never even been willing to take off the shelf. She'd heard of the book, but had been repulsed by her instant sexual stimulation and had refused to even entertain reading it. Even once she'd come to Bibliophile she'd avoided it like the plague. It seemed too much like crossing a line she'd never be able to come back from.

Her eye landed on the spine like it was a lodestone, and her breath hitched just a little as she reached for it. She quickly flipped it into her hand, grabbed a few other standard romances off the shelf that she'd wanted as well, and headed back to the sitting area to browse her books before buying.

Evan's gut clenched as the tinkle of Claire's laughter reached him in the store room where he was checking in the shipment that had arrived earlier that day. The sound raced through his veins like a bullet. It burned through him before settling in his cock, which twitched and lengthened painfully. This was not how this was supposed to go.

Damn it! He smacked the wall hard and focused on the searing pain that reverberated through his joints. She was just supposed to feel welcome back in the store. He wasn't supposed to start lusting after her again.

The pain began doing its job, and his cock deflated. He took several deep breaths, grabbed a stack of new releases that he wanted for the front window and, squaring his shoulders, opened the door and stepped out to meet his personal hell, only to have his entire body betray him once again.

She looked phenomenal. Whoever it was that she was dating, he apparently was treating her well. She looked radiant. Her hair was curling slightly around her face and she was dressed simply in a red, silk halter dress that set off her skin and made her seem like a siren come to call him to his doom. His gut clenched hard in the knowledge that he very much wanted to go to his doom with her.

She was, however, reading a book upside down and holding it like it was going to fly out of her hands if she relaxed her grip. His entire body deflated just like that. She was still out of sorts because of him. On that thought, Evan took a deep breath and blew it out slowly before walking over to the sitting area and setting his stack of books down on the table. Her knuckles went snow white around the book she was holding, and he heard a distinctly sharp indrawn breath. Not a good sign.

He settled his tall frame into the chair facing Claire, and waited for her to look at him. And waited. And waited. She never took her eyes off the book she clearly could not be reading. She just sat there, unmoving, the book clenched in her hand like a talisman of protection, and said nothing. Finally, he conceded defeat.

"Claire." He spoke softly, feeling like he'd spook her if he spoke too loudly. She didn't acknowledge him at first, just continued to ignore him. The moment dragged to the point where he'd gladly have peeled off his own skin, but he knew she'd heard him. Then, finally, he saw her take a deep breath and squeeze her eyes briefly before raising them to meet his. The wariness he saw there made his heart sink.

"Claire," he started again, leaning just a bit forward as he spoke, "I owe you an apology."

For a brief moment, the entire world shifted, then righted itself. The last thing Claire had expected to hear coming out of Evan's mouth was an apology. For several long moments, all she could do was stare at him as if he spouted horns and a tail. Whatever look was on her face, it must have amused him, because a slow grin spread across his face. The effect a simple smile from him, the first she'd ever received, had on her heart rate made the Energizer Bunny seem like it moved at a snail's pace.

Recovering herself, she said the only thing that came to her mind. "For what?"

Confusion crossed his face briefly, then he laughed. Again, the first she'd ever gotten from him. His laughter skittered across her skin, raising goose bumps and causing her womb to clench. Her breathing caught just a little. The laughing, smiling man in front of her drew her like a magnet. She could feel herself leaning toward him just a little, trying to absorb as much of this new Evan into her skin as possible. She felt herself softening a bit, a smile playing about her lips.

"You aren't going to make this easy for me, are you?"

The question drew her out of her haze and brought her back to her senses. She settled back into the chair and was relieved to see that she hadn't totally embarrassed herself. She crossed her legs and rested her hands in her lap before answering.

"No." She linked her fingers together so she wouldn't fidget and looked him in the eye, studiously ignoring the little hitch in her belly at the melted chocolate of his gaze.

He laughed again, but she simply waited, doing her best to maintain his gaze as he looked steadily at her. "I apologize, Claire, for reading you the riot act the last time you were here as well as for making you feel unwelcome. My behavior was out of line. I acted like an ass."

He was tracing small circles on the arm of the chair even as he met her gaze. The smile was gone, replaced with a scowl.

"You look awfully scowly for an apology." Again, she spoke without thinking, and cringed at the teenage quality of her words.

He sighed deeply and his expression relaxed as he ran a hand through his hair, leaving him looking rumpled and chagrined. "I expect better of myself. I'm not usually so prickly."

"So why do I have the honor of bringing out all of your mean, then?" Claire was losing her shyness as the conversation progressed, and he responded openly to her questions.

"I'm not mean to you," he protested, sitting up straight and scowling again.

"You are the barest minimum of civilized to me." She refused to back down. "You laugh, smile, and joke with all other customers. Hell, with Bridget you're downright sweet and brotherly, but with me it's all polite civility." She held up a hand as he made to interject. "No, let me finish." She was relieved to see him settle back into the chair. "You don't owe me anything. You certainly are not required to be anything other than polite and civil to me. But what makes it so insulting is that it is *only* me. Why?"

She drew in a breath as if to continue, but realized that was all she wanted to know. Why was he so different with her? If it was about that first night, then it was time to address it. She was through being places she wasn't wanted, but he was going to have to come out with it. Settling back in the chair, she crossed her legs, smoothed the silk over her thighs, and simply waited for him to speak.

He opened his mouth then closed it, only to repeat the process once more before finally just shaking his head and laughing. "I have no idea what to make of you, you know that?" When she just raised an eyebrow at him, he continued. "You come in here like a lost puppy that first night. As if a wrong word would send you scrambling. Then you proceed to work the reading club like you're a schoolteacher lecturing on the nuances of voice and figurative language, yet you fall asleep here and seem like you need a keeper." He looked toward the front of the store as he paused. A distant, pained look crossed his face and his fist clenched. When he looked back at her, his visage was ravaged, with what she didn't know, and his voice dropped as he choked out, "You confound me and…I'm uncomfortable with that. I'm used to knowing—no, that's not the right word—to being confident in my reactions to the people around me and you…you just don't fit into any molds I'm used to."

She didn't know what to say. There seemed to be much, much more to what he was saying than the words he was using. He roamed her face as if he was searching for the answer to a riddle and it was stamped on her features somewhere.

Before she could respond, he locked gazes with her and asked, "What brings you here, Claire? Why do you spend so much time here?"

Claire hadn't expected the question and she responded without thinking.

"I feel safe here." She waved a hand around to encompass the bookstore. "You make me feel safe. Despite your attitude, I don't believe you would hurt me." Claire flushed such a sweet shade of pink as she spoke, her hazel gaze roaming the store as she looked everywhere but at him.

Safe. She thought she was safe with him. That he wouldn't hurt her. Evan sat in stunned silence for the briefest moment before a red tide of fury suffused his body.

Fury at Marianne for dying and leaving him alone when she had been the center of his life. Fury at Claire for tempting him and reviving desires that he'd believed were dead and buried with his love. Fury at himself for being so damned foolish and afraid in the face of his temptation. In that moment, he knew himself for a coward and he snapped.

"Safe. You think you're safe with me?" he all but sneered at her. "You know nothing." He spit the words at Claire as he leaned forward, his hands clenched into fists on his knees. She shrank away from him, pushing so far back into the club chair her feet no longer touched the floor. Her eyes were wide with shock and the beginnings of fear. Shame crawled over his skin and he reached for self-control, only to lose it all over again when her small, white teeth bit into her trembling lower lip.

"Damn you!" He slammed a fist down on the arm of his chair, causing her to jump at the violence of his action. "You are anything but safe with me. Every time you walk through that door all I can think about is bending you over my lap and spanking that pretty little ass until it is shiny, red, and stinging. Then fucking you from behind so that the sting feeds the orgasm I give you. I fantasize about binding you and whipping those sweet little tits, your pussy, and your ass. Marking you everywhere so that each time you look in the mirror you remember me and how I put them there, and then beg me to put more on you when they heal. I want to drench you in my come, fuck you in every goddamn hole, and make you scream until you can't speak."

As the words died on his lips, he dragged in a breath and took

Claire in, really saw her now that the apex of his anger had passed somewhat. She was glassy-eyed and panting. The knuckles of her slim, elegant fingers were white and she gripped the arms of her chair as if her life depended on it. She looked like she was having a panic attack.

Fear and shame overrode his anger and he lurched forward, coming around and sitting on the table before her. He took her face between his palms. She was so tiny, his hands seemed to swallow her up.

"Claire." He spoke softly, soothingly, as he rubbed his thumb over her cheeks. "Claire, please. Look at me."

She turned just a fraction, closing her eyes and refusing to look at him. Her motion brought his thumb to rest on her lower lip. Quickly, so quickly he almost missed it, she licked his thumb. It was the barest touch, but the sight of her pink tongue against his skin was more than he could take. What control remained to him was lost.

"Damn you," he repeated, but this time it was the hoarse whisper of a drowning man. "Suck it," he demanded as he thrust his thumb between her full, rosy lips. She obeyed instantly, enveloping the digit in wet, velvet heat. A shudder coursed through him at the silken feel of her mouth on his skin. She sucked gently in slow draws that he felt all the way to his cock, which surged violently to life.

With his other hand he untied the bow that held the halter of her dress together and yanked the barrier from her body so that it pooled at her waist in a lake of red silk. She faltered briefly, but continued to suck on his thumb as he squeezed her breast, massaging and shaping it in his large palm. She was small, tiny even; the entire globe barely filled his palm, but his mouth watered to taste her. He pulled his thumb from her mouth and trailed damp circles around each nipple before leaning down to suck the puckered tips into his mouth. He sucked hard, eliciting a cry of pained pleasure from her as she arched into his mouth.

He squeezed and pulled, sucked and bit at her nipples furiously, his mind blank except for the driving urge to mark her, claim her. Only when they were red and swollen, jutting out from the cream of her skin, did he leave her breasts. But he was far from done with her. He yanked her hips forward and roughly pushed the skirt of her dress up to her hips. She wore a brief, black silk thong which disappeared in a savage yank as he tore it from her. The fragile elastic snapped as easily as if it were an errant thread. He dropped the offending silk to the floor and threw her legs over the arms of the chair so that she was spread and open to him.

He didn't stop to appreciate the sight she made, though the memory would haunt him later. Her eyes were half-closed and glazed with desire. Her rosy lips were parted and damp from her tongue. Her small, tight breasts were swollen and tipped with hard, berry-red pebbles from his earlier feasting. The scarlet silk pooled at her waist, framing and showcasing her plump hips and drenched pussy. The damp curls were trimmed close, just a shade darker than the honeyed brown of her tousled hair. No, in that moment, he only took in the sandpaper dryness of his throat and the need to taste her.

He plunged his tongue into her folds, spearing into her channel and diving deep. The walls of her core convulsed around him, driving him further into mindless need. He pulled out and licked her from opening to clitoris, and gloried in the keening wail he elicited from her. She was panting hard, gasping unintelligible words as he worked her pussy, pushing her hard, giving her no time to do anything other than take what he gave her. Her unique scent of jasmine and feminine heat washed over him, watering his mouth and fueling the desire to drink her down. She thrashed and bucked, but he held her firm, interspersing deep thrusts into her pussy with soft licks, nips, and sucks of her clit until she screamed high and long. A wail of pleasure and ecstasy broke from her lips that was music to his ears and a sweet accompaniment to the driving percussion of her pussy as it clenched and throbbed around his tongue. She wrapped her legs around his neck and squeezed him to her as she shuddered under his touch. He lapped at her, softly now, determined to wring every ounce of pleasure from her.

Only when her legs slid limply from his shoulders to rest splayed on the chair cushion did he stop and look at her. Her eyes were dilated and passion-glazed, with pupils so wide that the hazel of her iris was almost indiscernible. The fear was gone, replaced by a look of dazed wonder. Her tongue darted out and wet her bottom lip, and she swallowed hard, as if her throat were dry. With no real conscious thought, Evan leaned in and plunged his tongue into her mouth. He plundered and tasted, absorbing the feel of those soft lips under his, the taste of the coffee she'd been drinking and the underlying sweetness that was Claire. She was kryptonite to his self-control.

He surged to his feet and wrenched his pants open, springing his rigid, aching cock free. He gripped her by the hair and wrenched her upright, causing her to gasp. He thrust his cock deep into her mouth, forcing her to accommodate his girth and length. She gagged briefly, but he held firm, and she relaxed and began to swallow against him and to move along his length. Claire sucked him voraciously as she moaned around his cock. The feel of her soft, warm tongue combined with the sweet suction of her mouth and throat beat at him. Each suck and pull served to build the tension in his groin and back, drawing the muscles up tight as his body surged with the need for release. He fought the pull, though. If he was going to be damned, he was going to go down fighting.

Tentative hands reached up to slip into his jeans and massage his ass. Small fingers gripped and stroked and squeezed in syncopation with the hot suck of her mouth. When she scraped her teeth along his cock at the same time as she raked her nails along his ass, he broke. Gripping her hair hard, he thrust deep, threw back his head, and roared his release. With each thick, warm jet he spilled every fantasy, every unsatisfied hard-on, every frustrated desire he'd experienced since she'd begun to frequent his shop down her throat. She swallowed again and again, drawing every drop of pleasure from his body. She drank him down like it was the sweetest nectar and she an addict to the flavor.

He shook from the force of his release. She held his softening cock between lips now swollen and red. As he slipped wetly from her mouth, she rested her forehead against his lower belly and placed a soft, gentle kiss on his groin. The loss of her heat left him feeling bereft and ashamed for his loss of control. He remembered the fear in her eyes and squeezed his own shut against the lance of pain and recrimination that shot through him at the memory.

He reached down and tilted her chin up to look at him. Her eyes were wary again and swimming with tears that traced down her cheeks in crystal rivers. He caught one on his fingertip and rubbed it away. "Claire—"

At that moment, the chime from the front door sounded and she scrambled back from him. With hurried, jerky movements she yanked her dress into place and secured the top. Swiping at the tears on her face, she snatched her purse up and ran for the door.

"Claire," he hissed at her. "Wait." If she heard him, she gave no indication. She just slammed through the front door without a backward glance.

Evan tried to take in a deep breath against the agony squeezing his chest. What had he just done?

"Hello? Is anybody here?" A thin, high, feminine voice called from the area in front where the cash register was.

"Yes." Evan cleared his throat when the word came out as a croak and tried again. "I'll be right there."

He shoved his dick back in his pants and stooped to pick up the remnants of Claire's thong. He brought the scrap of silk to his nose and inhaled the soft, feminine musk that was now forever seared into his senses. Shoving the fabric into his pocket, he went to help his customer and try to marshal his thoughts and find some order in the maelstrom of emotions surging through him.

He reached for the stack of books he'd left on the table and only then did the book she'd been reading draw his attention. Fuck! His heart clenched hard even as his cock wanted to come back to life. It was *The Story of O.* The quintessential story of submission. Fuck! Fuck! *Fuck!*

Chapter 9

KNOCK. KNOCK. KNOCK.

The sound of the brass knocker on the loft's door startled Claire out of her sullen wallow. No one visited her without calling first. Hell, no one visited her. Period. The last thing she wanted was to deal with a stranger right now. Her nerves were still vibrating after what had happened with Evan. Not even a shower and a shot of whiskey had calmed her.

Maybe if she ignored them they'd go away. She pulled her robe tighter and hunched over on the sofa, where she perched with her arms wrapped around her knees and rocked back and forth.

Knock. Knock. Knock.

So much for them going away. If anything, they were getting more insistent. Chester had made his way over to the door and was snuffling and mewling a bit. At least he wasn't barking. She might still be able to get away with pretending to be out.

"Claire!" Evan's deep baritone sounded through the heavy steel door.

At the sound of his voice, Claire's heart set up a pounding rhythm that stole her breath. Her heart was thunking in her rib cage like an inmate at the penitentiary demanding freedom. Her limbs went liquid as she shuffled to the door. Her stomach twisted in a knot and her chest constricted. Breathing was becoming next to impossible. Her hand was surprisingly steady as she opened the door.

The sight that greeted her, however, was not reassuring. Evan filled the doorframe, looking anything but happy. Grim. That was the word. He looked like he was facing a firing squad.

"Evan?" She knew she was gaping, but she was stunned. "Why are you here? Wait? How did you even know where I lived?" Her voice was growing shrill as her nerves reasserted themselves.

"May I come in, Claire?" His voice was flat and low and he didn't meet her eyes.

"Why?" She still couldn't wrap her mind around him being at her door.

He squeezed his eyes closed and huffed out an exasperated breath before saying, "Because this isn't a conversation we need to be having in your hallway."

Claire's blood went cold at that statement. What in the hell could he possibly intend to say to her? She didn't bother to speak as she moved aside and waved him in. He stopped short as Chester made his presence known, but to his credit he just stood there and let the dog sniff until he gave a satisfied snort and went to lie on his bed at the end of the cream, leather sofa. Evan took up residence in one of the red, suede club chairs that flanked her sofa at either end of the antique chest she used as a coffee table. He set something on the chest and then settled back into the chair and, finally, looked directly at her.

His dark chocolate eyes were almost black, and the grimness was even more pronounced as she noted lines of stress that hadn't been there earlier. He was wearing the same clothes he'd worn before and looked as if he'd just come from the shop, which, from a quick glance at the clock on the cable box, would have closed about forty-five minutes before.

"Please sit down, Claire." He waved vaguely in the direction of her couch.

She felt rooted to the spot she was standing on. Some strange misgiving washed across her and made her want to walk the other way, not toward him. It was only then that she comprehended what he'd placed on the table. It was her book. The one she'd planned to take as her prize. *The Story of O.*

She remained where she was and felt the heat suffuse her body as she flushed deeply. He knew. Knew that she was exploring submission. Oh. Jesus Christ. How could he not after what she'd done in the store?

"Claire." Evan's voice was soft but firm, and her eyes snapped to his. "Sit down."

His tone brooked no argument, and this time she complied, moving to her sofa and sitting deliberately in the very middle so that she was as far away from him as was reasonable, but close enough that they could talk in normal tones. She started to reach for the book, but dropped her hand into her lap instead.

"Evan, why are you here? And how did you find me?" She couldn't wait for him to continue at this point. She was bursting with nervous energy.

"First, you're registered at the shop; I have your address in the system. As for why am I here…I've been asking myself that question the whole way over here." His tone was distracted and he was staring off toward the door. "I think this conversation is way past overdue, but I'm not at all sure how to have it."

"Look," Claire interjected. She didn't want to wait for him to let her down easily. She didn't need the rejection. "About what happened at the store. You don't need to concern yourself—"

She stopped abruptly as Evan narrowed his eyes and drew his eyebrows together in a fierce scowl.

"I don't need to concern myself with what, Claire?" he asked in a low, harsh voice. It was as if all that smoky scotch had just frozen. "The fact that I took advantage of you? Or the fact that you submitted to me?"

Hearing him voice the true nature of that act caused her body to go into hyperdrive. She could feel her nipples tightening and the flesh of her pussy quivering, but she was determined to handle this like an adult.

"Whether I…" She fluttered her hand in his direction, unable to say the words. So much for handling this like an adult. "You know or not," she continued lamely, pushing imaginary strands of hair out of her face, "is not relevant. The only thing that matters is that we handle ourselves like adults. You don't need to concern yourself—"

Claire fell back into the sofa as Evan growled and stood, snatching the book off the table and thrusting it in her direction.

"What exactly is your dom going to think about that little interaction? Hmm? Or are you planning on keeping it from him?" He stood over her, speaking through gritted teeth. His rib cage rose and fell with each tortured breath.

Claire gaped at him as she tried to make heads or tails of the words. *Dom?* What in the hell?

"I have no idea what you are talking about."

Evan squeezed his eyes shut briefly, then looked directly at her. Claire had no idea what to make of the look of pain that crossed his face. When he spoke again it was with the tortured slowness of an adult talking with someone who was a bit slow. The anger that began to burn in Claire's belly was anything but slow, however.

"The man you're seeing? Given your propensity for D/s erotica"—he waved the book in her face again—"I'm assuming this man is your dom. Were you my sub, I'd expect you to be telling me everything with no exceptions. So again, I ask you, are you going to tell him and, in which case, how do I not have to concern myself with overstepping such a boundary?"

All hesitancy left Claire as she realized the gross assumptions he was making. He could be such an ass! Shooting to her feet, she pulled herself up as straight as she could manage in light of her petite stature to his gargantuan size and said, with as much dignity as she could muster, "You're a complete ass, you know that?"

Evan's eyes went wide and his mouth gaped just a little bit as Claire's unexpected response registered.

"Sit down and listen." Claire pointed at the chair he had vacated and was immensely relieved when he cooperated, albeit very reluctantly. "You have absolutely no idea what the hell you are talking about. Why is it that you make so many fucking assumptions where I'm concerned yet can't be bothered to ask one fucking question?" She caught the raised eyebrow at her colorful language, but she really didn't care. "Drop your eyebrow. I know I'm cursing, but you've really pissed me off. Again."

She stopped and took a deep breath to calm herself down. It wouldn't do any good to just rail at him; she needed to ratchet it back. Returning to her seat on the sofa, she continued, "I am not seeing anyone and I don't have a dom. So you *don't* need to concern yourself with anything. OK? Got it?"

He didn't answer but just looked at her, his face unreadable for long, uncomfortable moments. She refused to give in to the urge to fill the silence, and returned his gaze despite the fact that it felt as if all her secrets were writing themselves across her forehead like one of those scrolling, digital tickers they had on all the news shows.

Finally, he tilted his head slightly in the direction of the table that backed up against her sofa and said, "Who is he then?" He indicated a photo of Claire and Marcus that she'd only recently added to the collection of knickknacks and framed photos of Chester that adorned the table. "I've seen you with him."

Something in the tone of those words had Claire's eyes shooting back to Evan's face, but she saw nothing. Not one little twitch of an eye muscle even. Well, two could play the "you can't read me" game.

Schooling her face to blankness, she said, "That's Marcus." She waited two beats, just enough time to take a small pleasure in the narrowing of Evan's eyes, and added, "My brother."

His eyes flared briefly before he schooled them back to

impassivity and said, "Your brother. You two must be very close then. I mistook you for lovers the night I saw you at dinner."

Claire almost laughed out loud, but she saw that he was completely serious and, again, something in his tone warned her now was not the time to push him too far. He seemed—raw.

"At Luna Bella?" she asked, and took his sharp nod as confirmation. "I hadn't seen Marcus in ten years before that night. That was a reunion of sorts." Her voice trailed off as she thought back to that night and how good it had felt to reconnect with Marcus; she didn't try to control the smile playing around her lips. "Yes, I guess we were rather affectionate given the circumstances."

"So you aren't seeing anyone?"

She shook her head.

"Answer me properly, Claire." The words came out clipped and sharp.

Claire felt her body respond immediately to Evan's command. She squeezed her thighs a bit more tightly and considered whether to answer him or not. She knew if she did she was taking a step down a path that *she* wanted, but she wasn't at all sure he did.

"No, I'm not seeing anyone."

Evan's lips quirked briefly, but he said only, "And you have no dom?"

"No, I don't have a dom."

"But you want one." This last was no question. She remained silent.

"Answer me, Claire."

Her eyes snapped once again to his, but she said only, "I fail to see what business of yours that is."

"The minute you submitted to me in my store it became my business. Do you think submission is a joke? Something to be taken lightly?"

"No." Her chin rose a smidge higher as she strove to rein in her growing annoyance. "I do not. If I did, I would have already found a willing man to dominate me, I'm quite sure."

"You've been looking." Again, not a question. He really was quite arrogant.

"No." She didn't elaborate.

"But you want a dom." She remained silent.

"Answer me, Claire."

"No. You are not my dom; I do not owe you my obedience. So you answer me. Why do you care?" She was fuming now. "You show up on my doorstep and start drilling me on things that are none of your business. You *tell me why* or I don't answer shit." She crossed her arms over her chest, even knowing how childish it seemed. Evan's laugh caught her completely off guard.

He leaned forward, chuckling and shaking his head as he rested his elbows on his knees. "OK. Fair enough." Taking a deep breath, he ran a hand through his hair, leaving him tousled and sexy as ever, but it was his words that stole her breath. "I've been watching you and even making sure to leave out selections for you to read. After what happened in the store, I'm convinced more than ever you are a submissive, but you need a dom to take you down this path. You say you don't have one. I'm offering to be that dom and teach you what you need to know."

What in the fuck had he just said? That was not what he came here to do. He came here to set things straight between them. To apologize for his loss of control. To put to rest this weirdness between them once and for all. And now he was offering to dominate her? To initiate her into BDSM?

He waited for the pain, the suffocating grief, the recriminations, but he felt strangely blank. Maybe he was supposed to do this? He *was* very concerned for her safety if she was poorly initiated. It didn't have to be sexual. It could just be about teaching her. He didn't have to fuck her.

He wouldn't fuck her. Yes! He wouldn't fuck her.

"Did you hear me?" Claire's voice broke into his rationalizations. He took in the confused look on her face.

"Huh?" He could've smacked himself. Great recovery.

"I said"—she cocked her head to one side, giving him a speculative glance—"did you hear me?"

"No." He saw no use in dissembling. "My thoughts ran away with me."

"So, I'm supposed to let a man dom me who can't even keep his concentration in a basic conversation?" That stung.

"Sit properly and pay attention." The order was snapped out in a flat tone; he didn't even raise his voice, but was very pleased that she instinctively complied.

He could see the look of consternation on her face at having responded to the command, but he refrained from giving in to the urge to smile. She was testy with him, and rightfully so.

"Lesson number one. A dominant is not without flaws. In my case, I sometime wander in thought, but this is not a scene. During a scene, my number-one focus is on you and the scene in play. Breaks in concentration are not acceptable and if they occur the scene needs to end." She didn't respond, but seemed to absorb what he was saying. "Now, please, repeat what you said."

"I asked why you would want to dom me. This seems like a very sudden change on your part and I generally don't trust sudden changes in anyone's demeanor."

"A reasonable question." He hesitated for a moment, eying her defensive posture and closed air. Taking a deep breath, he continued, "Claire, in order to even have this conversation you and I need to establish at least one ground rule. OK?"

"Depends on what it is."

Damn, but she was stubborn. There were ways to deal with that, though. Evan clamped down ruthlessly on the stirring in his cock at the image of Claire turned over his knee, her naked ass up in the air waiting for a spanking. *Concentrate!* This was not about sex.

"Honesty. The foundation of any relationship is honesty, but in BDSM it is even more critical because of the potential for physical and emotional harm involved. If you and I are going to have this conversation, there can't be any dishonesty between us. You may not know the answer to a question and that's fine, but I need you to tell me what you believe to be true and honest to the best of your ability and I will do the same."

Her eyes narrowed at him for several seconds before she gave a sharp nod. "OK. Agreed."

"OK, I'll start." She only raised an eyebrow, but it practically shouted "Duh!" and he couldn't help but chuckle, which only drove that eyebrow higher. "I have been watching you since you first came into Bibliophile. You screamed fragile. I reacted to that in a way that made me uncomfortable."

Her eyes went wide, but he continued.

"You see, I haven't been in any kind of BDSM relationship since my wife died. She was my submissive for ten years and I still love and miss her. Having my dom instincts revived at any level didn't sit well with me. It's been the reason for my distance with you. I don't want to enter into any kind of relationship and I didn't want to encourage you or lead you on accidentally."

Claire let out a very inelegant snort, but she didn't interrupt.

"I inadvertently overheard a conversation you had with Bridget while I was shelving some books and realized that you might have masochistic tendencies and with the erotica you were reading—but refusing to buy; yes, I noticed, by the way—that you were curious about dominance and submission. I started leaving out books for you to read. I've known women like you—" He held up a hand to forestall any protest.

"That's not a judgment; now be still and let me finish." He

took a deep breath and continued, "A lot of women have the same tendencies you do and do exactly what you did, get involved in a very dysfunctional and dangerous situation for all involved. I wanted you to see that you could explore your obvious desire for pain in a controlled environment. When I saw you with your brother, I thought you'd begun to date someone and was concerned about your initiation to BDSM. If it's done wrong it can do irreparable damage. Given that you've indicated you are not actually involved, I'm offering to dom you. To introduce you to BDSM."

"You still haven't explained your recent assholishness with me."

It was his turn to raise an eyebrow and give her a hard look at the insult, but she didn't back down. In his military days, he'd had enlisted men cower before him for less. He had to give her credit for her gumption. He'd work on that cheekiness with him too.

"Assholishness isn't a word." She just shrugged and waited.

He sighed and ran a hand through his hair. She really was stubborn. "I was unhappy at the possibility of you being harmed. You bring out all of my protective instincts and I wasn't prepared for that. In truth, I still find it a bit uncomfortable. The reality, Claire, and this I have to be 100 percent clear on, is that I am offering to dom you, but not to fuck you."

She flinched at the crudity but never dropped her eyes.

"Why do it then?"

"BDSM doesn't have to be sexual. There are many partners who practice dominance and submission or other aspects of BDSM play who never have sex. BDSM is an exploration of the sensual in all of its forms, not necessarily the sexual, though for many sex and BDSM go together. This is the offer I'm making. Whether you accept it or not is up to you. You don't have to answer me right now. You might want to take some time to think about it."

She gave him a hard look and he could almost see the wheels turning in her mind.

"No sex?"

"No sex."

"You'll teach me about BDSM? Initiate me?"

"Yes."

"How would you go about it?"

"Well, that's a question that requires a lot more thought than off the top of my head, but at the highest level, we'll do a lot of talking about your needs, your desires, your cravings, and your pain and other baggage that you're carrying."

"Why that?"

"I'll need to know as much about you as possible to make sure I make the right decisions as we go about this."

She seemed to want to ask more, but remained silent.

"Claire." His voice was soft, and she met his eyes. The worried hope he saw in them tore at his heart. "You don't have to give me an answer right now. In truth, I think you shouldn't. You need to really think this over. Here's what I want you to do. And this is a suggestion since you have not agreed to be my sub. OK?"

He waited for her to respond. She nodded.

"Here's my personal email and cell phone number." He pulled out a business card and wrote the necessary info on the back. "Call me or email me with any questions. In the meantime, I want you to read this book." He pushed *The Story of O* across the chest to her. "Think hard about if you really want to go down this path. If you find your answer is yes, then we'll share a coffee after your next book club meeting and talk. OK?"

Flooded hazel eyes roamed his face as if searching for something. Deception? Sincerity? He wasn't sure, but he let her look her fill. Finally, she said, "OK."

Evan stood and with a brief, "I'll see myself out," he left her loft. If only the image of her freshly showered, wrapped in that delicate robe, looking at him like he might just be the answer to her prayers had stayed on the sofa with her.

Claire pulled her robe closer around her as she stared after Evan. She couldn't decide if the quivery feeling low in her belly was fear, hope, or arousal. If she were being completely honest, it was most likely equal parts of all three. The idea of Evan, the living embodiment of her fantasies, becoming her dom was more than she could have ever hoped for.

The idea of him doing to her all the things that she read about… She clapped a hand to her breast as her heart raced in anticipation and fear. Could she handle it?

That was the ever-present question. Could she handle it? But did she even truly know what she was getting herself into? No, she didn't. She guessed this was where the talking and reading would come in. Her eyes strayed to the book on her table. No time like the present.

Grabbing the book and one of the colorful pillows adorning the couch, she tucked it behind her head. With a quick "here, boy," she called Chester up to snuggle with her and opened the cover.

Chapter 10

CLAIRE OPENED THE DOOR to Bibliophile and felt both as if she'd come home and entered an alien abode. Everything was as it always had been. Neat. Tidy. Welcoming and redolent of coffee and chocolate chip cookies. But never had she walked into this store with the knowledge that she would be spending time with Evan when the meeting was done. Or that Evan would be willing to do all manner of things to her to educate her in the ways of BDSM. Her breath hitched as the thought crossed her mind. What would he be like with her after that last conversation? She had no way of knowing whether she was about to get Evan who was willing to dom her or growly, stay away from me Evan.

The last few days had been ones of anticipation. She hadn't emailed or called him, not feeling comfortable enough to do that yet. She had, however, made a list of questions she wanted to ask him during their chat after the meeting. Claire had no idea how she was going to get through this meeting, but get through it she would. *Please, please, please let Jean pick someone else to lead the discussion.* As it was, Claire had just finished the book in question, Christine Feehan's *Deadly Game*, that morning.

Evan stepped out of the stacks as she progressed to the meeting space and smiled at her. Her heart bottomed out at that smile. He'd always avoided any kind of interaction with her. She might get a perfunctory nod from him, but a smile…This was a first and her body was acting as if he'd kissed her—melting and turning liquid—rather than just smiled at her in greeting.

She smiled back, completely forgetting to keep moving until a tap on the shoulder unlocked her body. Turning, she had only a split second to register a welcoming grin before she was enveloped in Bridget's hug.

"It's good to have ya back, darlin'," Bridget said after releasing Claire.

"It's good to be back," Claire said, a grin splitting her face.

They made their way to the back of the store, chatting as they went.

"I want all the dirt," Bridget said as they settled into two adjacent folding chairs.

"Dirt on what?" Claire asked in confusion.

Bridget snorted loud enough to draw the attention of some of the other attendees who were assembling quickly.

"I saw Evan smile at you, hon." She dipped her head in a decisive nod. "That's a huge change from Mr. I-Barely-Acknowledge-You. So I want to know what happened."

Claire smiled. She couldn't help herself. "Well, so far there isn't really a lot to tell, but there might be."

Whatever Bridget was about to say was forestalled as Jean called the meeting to order, but the look in her eyes told Claire that the conversation wasn't quite over.

"Welcome, everyone." Jean's cheerful lilt rang out among the assembled members. "You'll notice the lovely Claire has rejoined our ranks." She waved a hand in Claire's direction, and there was a round of murmured welcomes to which she just smiled and nodded. "Claire," Jean addressed her directly, "I'm assuming you read *Deadly Game*?"

"Yes." She smiled brightly, only to have it falter at Jean's reply.

"Good then. Take it away." Jean's grin was almost evil.

Mentally, Claire groaned, but take it away she did.

"Be careful and don't rush into anything." Bridget's words were soft in Claire's ear as she hugged her.

"I will. Promise." Claire squeezed her back hard before retaking her seat at the back of Bibliophile.

She knew Bridget meant well and, truthfully, she was right. Too many people rushed into BDSM. Especially girls who thought they were submissive. They hooked up with the first man who claimed to be a dominant and willing to show them the ropes in some kind of sub-frenzy. As if the realization that they were submissive meant it was okay to submit to just anyone.

In one of those ass-backward twists of the universe, Claire's inherent distrust and skepticism had protected her so far. She'd signed up on Fetlife, a kinky social network, and had closed the account down within a month. All she'd gotten was bombarded with so-called doms demanding she engage in some form of online submission with them or meet up with them so she could submit in person. Or, her favorite, she'd received random cock shots from men despite the fact her profile had been very clearly labeled that she only wanted to learn more and be "friends."

The self-proclaimed doms had given no reasonable rationale for why she should submit to them. It was generally "because I said so," which only proved to make her even more reticent. The more she waited and lurked in the forums, the more she saw posts about safe words being ignored, or this dom or that abusing someone. It had proven to her exactly how careful you had to be in choosing to submit to someone.

Truthfully, she was still taking a risk with Evan. They weren't even in a traditional relationship. They'd had very little in the way of interaction. All she had was Bridget's recommendation of him as a person and his own word. She would proceed with caution. Which was exactly why, despite her embarrassment, she'd come clean to Bridget about what she was considering. She also planned to tell Evan that Bridget was aware.

She might be volunteering to be the submissive in this relationship, but that didn't equate to giving up all personal responsibility for herself or common sense. If anything, her responsibility to look out for herself was even greater than it would be normally due to the possible ramifications to her body and psyche. This was not something to be blithely walked into. In fact, Evan was auditioning for his role as dom as much as she was for sub.

"Claire?"

The sound of her name on Evan's lips dripped across her skin like honey and she gave a little shiver. She set the magazine she was browsing through down. She was entirely too wound up tonight to read a book.

"Hi." Her own voice came out a bit breathless and whispering. He smiled at her, once again sending little shivers down her spine. She really needed to get a grip on herself. She was responding like a starry-eyed teenager rather than the grounded woman she was.

"I'm just going to close up and then we can go grab a bite to eat."

Disappointment flooded her, a bit unreasonably, she supposed. What exactly had she expected? Him to Harry Potter a St. Andrew's Cross in the middle of the store and flog her until she came?

Pulling on a smile, she nodded and said, "OK. Sounds good to me."

Evan gave her a hard look. "What was our first ground rule?"

Confusion replaced the disappointment. "What? I'm not sure—"

"In your loft. Our first ground rule. What was it?" His voice wasn't harsh or even cold; it was just flat. In some ways, that was worse.

Claire thought back for a second and said, "Honesty. There must be complete honesty."

Evan nodded, but his expression didn't change. "That's still in effect. So explain the fake smile regarding dinner."

Claire flushed bright red. She could feel it suffusing her skin and heating her flesh. Damn, she hadn't thought he could read her that easily.

"It's nothing, really." He just raised an eyebrow and she rushed on, "I just was surprised by the idea of us going to dinner considering…" She trailed off and waved a hand between them.

Evan took the seat immediately to her right and leaned in toward her, dropping his voice a bit. "Claire, if you can't even say the words, what makes you think you're ready to even explore this?" His voice was kind, the flatness gone, but somehow that bothered her more.

"I can say the words, Evan." She lifted her chin a notch as she met his gaze. "I might need to get over my natural shyness at discussing something so private with a man I barely know, but I can say the words."

"Say them, then."

"I thought we were going to discuss whether or not you and I would pursue my submission to you and my exploration of BDSM, not go to dinner. And, by the way, I decided to tell Bridget everything. So she knows what I'm discussing with you."

Evan's grin hit her full in the chest, "You did, did you? That was smart." The approval in his eyes gave her such a melting feeling inside. It was as if knowing she'd pleased him filled a space in her heart she didn't even know needed filling. "I'm taking us to dinner, first, because we need to eat and, second, it will take a little of the pressure off for our conversation and it will be good to do it in neutral space. My apartment is upstairs, but I think that sends the wrong message for our first conversation, as would your loft, and I keep this part of my life separate from my business."

At his words, Claire felt her chest ease, and she closed her eyes. She hadn't even realized how nervous she was at the idea of really embarking on this conversation with him. She'd fantasized relentlessly about him since the first time she'd walked through his door and, with the possibility of all her fantasies becoming real, she felt almost frenetic as the time drew closer.

She jumped as Evan took her hand in his and slowly rubbed his thumb over the back of her hand. In a calm, even voice he said, "Claire, look at me."

She raised her eyes to his and, for a moment, felt as if she melted right into the liquid chocolate of his eyes.

"This is just a conversation. There are no strings. No obligations. No requirements for you to submit to me in any way tonight. You have complete control of how far we take this. At every step along the way, even if we proceed to actual BDSM play, you will have the ultimate control. It will be your choice if we continue, your choice to submit, and your choice to stay. Submitting to me doesn't remove your control over your life, it only establishes the terms of our interaction while we have it. Understand?"

Her throat squeezed at his intuitive knowledge of her fears. The lack of control over her life. She wanted to submit sexually to a man. She wanted to experience some of the other forms of play. She did not want to lose the ultimate control of her life by default.

Tears welled in her eyes and she squeezed his hand where he still held hers. "Thank you, Evan."

"You OK?" Gentle eyes roamed her face, looking for confirmation.

"Yes, I'm fine." Her smile was shaky, but it was the best she could do. "Promise."

"OK." He gave a firm nod and released her hand. "Give me a few minutes to close out and lock up."

Standing, he moved toward the cash register to complete whatever he did to close out the store. Claire was quite pleased to see she wasn't so freaked out that she couldn't appreciate the sight of his tight ass in those jeans as he moved off.

She glowed in the candlelight. Her creamy skin appeared almost translucent and the soft reflection cast enough shadows that her eyes seemed huge and luminescent. Her hair floated around her face, making her seem almost angelic—and it was really time to pull back from channeling Hallmark. He wasn't here to write odes to Claire as the innocence-enshrouded libertine of his reluctant fantasies. He was here to talk to her seriously about whether or not she was truly ready to explore submission and impact play.

"Claire." He waited for her to look at him. "Relax. Please."

Her hands, which had been restlessly picking at the linen table-cloth, stilled and she rested them on either side of her plate. He'd brought her to Chance, a local midscale eatery, where their jeans would fit right in, but the food was still exquisite. Not that you could tell from the way she was picking at her lobster ravioli, and she'd barely even sipped her wine.

"I'm sorry," she said, her voice low. "I just feel like I've got ants under my skin and I don't really know what to do with myself." She fidgeted even as she spoke. Her obvious tension was beginning to infect him. His stomach was going tight.

Reaching across the table, he took her hand. "Claire, look at me."

He waited as she met his eyes. What he saw in those hazel depths cut right through him. Fear. Pain. Hope. It was the hope that made him wish he could run away and hide from her. This tiny promise of doom sitting before him, waiting to be ravished, and he seemed not to be able to leave her alone.

"Take a deep breath." He waited as she closed her eyes and complied. "Now, talk to me. Why do you think that is?" She started to take her hand away, but he wouldn't let it go. When her eyes flew to his, he just smiled, shook his head briefly, and murmured, "Human contact is relaxing. It creates endorphins. Just relax."

She shifted her grip a bit and relaxed her hand in his. She dropped her gaze before looking off over his shoulder for several seconds prior to speaking. Her hand was surprisingly small and delicate, even more so than her petite stature might indicate. It was almost childlike and felt like satin in his palm. If the rest of her skin felt like her hands, it was going to be pure ecstasy to spank her. At the image of Claire bent over his knee, his cock made its presence known, and he involuntarily squeezed Claire's hand. Surprisingly, she squeezed back. He was about to apologize, but she finally started speaking.

"I first suspected I might be inclined toward BDSM after reading *Finding Herself* at Bibliophile, but you already know that." She sighed deeply and gave him a wry smile, and once again seemed to be searching for the right words. Finally, she shrugged and just looked helplessly at him. "I don't know how to talk to you about this."

"Stop thinking and just talk. Tell me about the beatings with Charlie." The flash of pain across her face tore at him, but this was important and needed to be discussed. "Stop thinking, just talk. And Claire"—again he waited for her to look at him—"the one thing I will never do is judge you." Tears welled in her eyes and, for a moment, he thought she'd break into sobs, but she took several deep breaths, squeezed her eyes tight for a few seconds and, with them still closed, began to speak.

"Charlie was always trying to get me to talk about my childhood and my relationship with my family, and I hated it." Her words were more a hiss than speech on that last bit. She opened her eyes and met his gaze. "Every conversation felt like being squeezed in a vice. As if the air were being sucked out of me and I was going to fold in on myself. I couldn't speak. I couldn't breathe. I would just want to run from him."

She shook her head as if to clear it.

"The more he pushed the more I resisted until I would, eventually, begin to lash out. I would take cheap shots at him. Disrespect him. Do any and everything that I knew he hated to push his buttons until he cracked and gave me what I wanted."

Her eyes had gone unfocused as she gazed off somewhere over his shoulder again.

"The physical pain was so much easier to take than the emotional. I have a very high pain tolerance. Sometimes I wouldn't even cry, but sometimes"—another deep, steadying breath—"sometimes, he would pull my hair really hard, hard enough to yank out strands, or punch me in just the right spot and I would cry. The tears were like having a floodgate open. Once I started crying, I wouldn't be able to stop. I'd cry and cry, but when the tears finally dried up, it was as if the vice inside me had been released. I could talk then. I could discuss my pain and my fear."

Evan didn't think she realized it, but her grip on his hand had become viselike. Were he a smaller man, it would have been painful. She was stronger than she looked. He said nothing, however, not wanting to redirect her attention.

"The problem was that Charlie hated what I was doing to him. He'd grown up watching his father beat his mother and he'd vowed never to do it. Unfortunately, I knew the chink in his armor"— she continued, her tone going flat—"and because I knew it, I could manipulate him with it. All I had to do was imply I was cheating on him. He hates the notion of being cuckolded. The more I made it seem like I was cheating, the easier his trigger was to pull. I craved those arguments. Not the beatings per se, they hurt. They scared me, but the crying, the release, the catharsis…I craved that and I didn't care if I hurt him to get it. Didn't see how I was destroying any hope for our relationship." She pulled her hand away from his and he let her this time.

"He hates me now." Her voice was a mere whisper as she finished.

"Thank you, Claire." His tone was gentle. "That couldn't have been easy to tell me. I'm proud of you for being that courageous." He saw, and was pleased at, the slight pink flush that suffused her skin. "Let's finish up, grab some coffees next door, and we'll take a walk. Right now, why don't you just tell me about Chester?"

Her entire face transformed at the mention of her Pit Bull Terrier. She obviously loved that dog. And while she couldn't seem to get out the words about wanting to be spanked or to feel pain just yet, she had no problem regaling him with tales of Chester. It was so sweet and she was so animated and happy talking about her dog, he felt a heartstring melt. *Fuck.*

———

Claire pulled the covers up tight around her neck as she snuggled into her bed. The dream she'd just woken from had left her wet and pulsing. Evan had made it very clear that they weren't looking at sex as part of the deal, but her subconscious was clearly ignoring him. Oh, he'd made her blush right to her roots when he'd indicated that he would reserve the right to bring her to orgasm regularly and often, but that he himself would not be partaking in her body. He was adamant that his heart still belonged to his wife and he was content that way.

She envied his love of his wife at the same time she pitied his inability to understand that life was for the living. To be so emotionally tied to someone who was lost forever to you made her ache for him.

Reflecting back on their conversation, she was certain she was making the right choice. She would gift her submission to Evan. He hadn't judged her. Hadn't made her feel like some kind of freak. The fact that he'd been the one leaving out all the books actually made her feel pretty cared for.

She would have to be very careful to keep her own feelings in perspective. It didn't take a genius to see that her feelings went deeper than infatuation. When he'd taken her hand over dinner and she'd looked in his eyes, she'd been confident she was going to embarrass herself by admitting how deeply she desired him, but she'd held it together.

Their walk had been enjoyable, and she'd found herself relaxing with him in ways she wouldn't have dreamed possible even a few weeks ago. She only hoped that when they had their first session, she would be able to stay calm and not disappoint either of them.

Chapter 11

IF HIS HANDS DIDN'T stop shaking, he was going to run amok. Evan considered the shot of bourbon he'd poured. As tempted as he was to indulge in a little liquid relaxation, that wouldn't do at all. He poured it out and took some deep breaths to calm his nerves. He'd done this hundreds of times with Marianne. There was no reason for him to be so wound up, but the idea of Claire here in his apartment was giving him butterflies like he hadn't experienced since he was a teenager and had asked Milly Fulbright to the Winter Dance his freshman year.

All of their "sessions" so far had been strictly talking. They'd take Chester for walks around town, go to the park, get coffee, all with the purpose and design of setting Claire's mind at ease and allowing them to get to know one another without the specter of BDSM hanging over their heads.

He didn't believe in dominating a woman he'd just met—at least, one with no experience whatsoever. He had negotiated scenes with experienced subs, but this was something completely different. Claire's initiation was not something to be taken lightly. In addition, he was taking an aspect of her psyche into his hands and if he screwed up she would be the one to carry that damage for the rest of her life.

He was experienced in impact play. It had been a regular part of his relationship with Marianne, but the way his nerves were acting up you'd think he'd never seen a flogger before. And spanking, hell, that was one of his all-time favorite things to do.

The image of a naked Claire draped over his lap, her sweet ass up in the air and waiting for him to turn it baby pink flashed in his mind, causing his cock to harden. That was exactly why his nerves were shot.

Talking with Claire, allowing her to share her hopes, her dreams, her fears, and her baggage was one thing. He'd found her to be an intelligent, funny, and deeply scarred woman who was her own worst enemy. She tortured herself over her past and still carried long-held beliefs of worthlessness and shame. Not that she'd admit to feeling worthless.

Despite all their talking, there was a wall they always came to. She became jumpy and agitated; she kept trying to change the subject. Talking became more about attrition than about her being open and it was time for that to change. Hence their meeting in his apartment today.

Today, Claire was getting spanked if she didn't open up voluntarily. The twitch in his crotch let him know his cock liked that idea very much. Evan wished he didn't agree. At the knock on his door, his chest clenched, and he had to take several deep breaths to relax.

A second knock had him double-timing it across the living room to his front door. As he opened it, he was not at all prepared for the sight that met his eyes. She was fucking radiant.

He was a wreck. He made roadkill seem fresh. All of Claire's happy fizzled. She'd been excited to come to his house, to see his personal domain and get a greater insight into the man with whom she'd been spending so much time. They mainly talked about her. She never got to really delve into him the way she wanted.

Spending time with him had proved to her that he was indeed the kind, compassionate man she'd believed him to be. He'd never once been judgmental of her. Never criticized or shamed her for the things she'd confessed to him. And through the reading he'd directed her to do along with their conversations she'd been able to reconcile so many of her desires with her "programming" around them, but he was still something of an enigma.

Right now, though, he looked like he'd had one too many sleepless nights, which made no sense since she'd seen him at the club meeting last night and he'd looked fine. Glancing past him, she spotted the bourbon bottle on the table and went rigid. Drunk was so not a part of this equation.

"Claire." His voice was tense. "Please come in."

She didn't move.

"Have you been drinking?"

He blanched but looked her in her eye and said, "No."

She searched his face for several seconds and, satisfied with what she saw, nodded briskly before stepping into his living room. His apartment was sparsely masculine. Clean and tidy. There wasn't much that gave away the man underneath the carefully controlled exterior. There was a bookcase in the corner and she would make an inspection of it, but right now she wanted to know what was going on with Evan.

Turning to face him, she said, "What is wrong?"

The muscles in Evan's jaw went rigid. "Claire, have a seat."

"No, thank you. I want to know what's going on."

"Claire, that wasn't a request."

"Evan, we aren't doing the D/s thing right now." She raised her chin and looked him directly in the eye. "We won't be doing it at all unless I'm satisfied that you are fit to participate with me right now."

Evan took a step closer to her and loomed large. She could smell the light, citrusy scent of his soap and his nearness was doing crazy things to her pulse, but she wasn't appreciating his attempts at intimidation right now.

Being her dom meant being in his right mind when they were

going to explore any kind of submission and he was not making her comfortable at the moment.

"Claire." He spoke in a commanding tone and her body went liquid at it, but she resisted. "I am telling you to sit down and we will talk."

She continued to look at him for several seconds and then said, "I'm going to sit down, but I'm doing it so we can talk, because I don't submit for no good reason. And right now, I'm not pleased. Got it?"

His laughter was like a cork popping off a champagne bottle; it startled her, but also gave her a little tingle before relaxing her as she absorbed it.

Taking a seat on the sofa, she said again, "Evan, you look like hell. I really need you to talk to me right now."

He came around and sat down on the far end of the sofa. It was as if he didn't want to be close to her and she felt a cut right through her heart.

"Claire, first, I need you to understand. I will never engage you in a scene of any kind if I've been drinking. I was seriously considering taking a shot, but I didn't."

While her tension eased a bit at his words, he wasn't answering her question.

"Why were you even considering it?"

He ran a hand through his hair, leaving him tousled and incredibly sexy. Her hands itched to smooth out his locks, but she refrained. Despite the time spent together, she still felt a bit hesitant with him.

With a deep sigh, he looked her dead in the face and said, "I'm nervous."

Claire had to consciously close her mouth. If you had given her a million years she would never have guessed Evan was nervous. Regretting his decision to dom her? Yes. Wishing she would just go away and leave him alone? Yes. Nervous? Hell no.

His smile was wry as he took in her obvious disbelief. "Yes, Claire. I'm nervous. It has been years since I've done a session with anyone and my one attempt after Marianne died didn't go well for me. It was agonizing to be with another woman." He looked down at the floor as he spoke to her. His elbows rested on his knees and his hands were loosely clasped. He projected a pensive air as he retreated into his past for several moments. "I'm not saying this to hurt or offend you in any way. I've already told you of my wife and our relationship, and, well—" He looked up at her. "Claire, you've been holding back. That stops tonight. You will comply with full and complete honesty or you will be spanked. Frankly, the idea of spanking you after so many years and with Marianne still so present in my heart has me nervous."

Her heart melted even as her pussy throbbed at the idea of Evan spanking her. She should probably be offended at the undercurrent of him wishing she were someone else, but how could she hold his dead wife against him? It wasn't as if he'd made any false promises to her so far.

"I understand, Evan." She made sure to face him and smile. "Thank you for telling me that. I admit, I've been very nervous myself with each conversation we've had. I've wondered when we would take the next step, but I'm confused. What makes you think I'm not being completely honest?"

"Claire." He raised an eyebrow. "Let's not start off with dissembling. You know exactly what I'm talking about."

"No, I don't." Her chin lifted a little higher.

He looked at her for a few moments before saying, "Let's take a step back for a moment. First, would you like something to drink?"

"No, thank you. I'm good."

"OK. Here's the deal. I want to know more about why you've treated yourself like a punching bag. I want to know what it was you were avoiding every time you manipulated Charlie into beating you."

Her stomach clenched at his words and her heart started racing. "But I already told you about that."

"No, Claire. What you've told me is the what—that you manipulated Charlie into beating you and that, once he did, you felt more able to communicate, but you've not explained the why. What were you avoiding confessing?"

"I was avoiding talking about my mother."

"Again, why?"

"I think I'll take that drink now."

"No."

Startled, she locked gazes with him. "What do you mean, no?"

"I mean, I'm not getting you a drink right now because that is deflection. You are attempting to redirect this conversation."

"No, I'm not."

"Now we're adding dishonesty." He stood, and her heart leaped into her chest. "Claire, I warned you. Stand up and put your hands on the chest."

"What?" She practically hollered the word.

He pointed at the chest. "Hands on the chest. For that bit of dishonesty, you've earned your first spanking."

She looked from him to the chest repeatedly, not sure if he was being serious.

"Claire." Her eyes snapped up to his. They were unfathomable. "I'm not going to fly off the handle and beat you. This is very calculated and controlled, but you are not going to hold back. Period. Now, you can comply or we can end this."

She didn't want to end this, but she sure as hell didn't want to get spanked either. Not like this. Not as punishment. She wanted to get spanked while having sex. This was definitely not about sex. With a shaky breath and a nod, she stood and bent over the chest, placing her hands firmly on the surface.

Evan moved behind her, and pushed her soft cotton skirt up

over her hips and slid her boy shorts down her thighs. Goose bumps pebbled on her skin as the cool air hit her. She shivered in the knowledge that she was bare before him and felt her core flood even as her breathing went ragged in anticipation of the pain.

Smack. Smack. A sharp, tingling sting radiated across each cheek and tears rushed to her eyes.

"Claire." Evan's voice was firm as he said, "Tell me what I want to know."

"I told you already."

Smack. Smack. The tingle got sharper and deeper and the tears were flowing freely now. Her skin throbbed and the sting spread across the entirety of her ass. He wasn't hitting her severely, but he wasn't being gentle either.

"What were you avoiding?"

She couldn't speak; she just closed her eyes against the tears and shook her head.

Smack. Smack. She jumped that time and tried to crawl across the chest, but he grabbed her hips and held her firm. She was sobbing openly now. Her ass burned and pulsed from the pain. Evan began to soothe her, rubbing her gently on the tender, heated skin before gently pulling her panties back up over her ass and dropping her skirt back into place. She heard him sit down on the couch and say, "Come here, baby."

It was the first time he'd called her anything other than Claire. She wasn't sure he was even aware of it, but she complied as he pulled her into his lap and held her as she sobbed. Her ass was sore, and the sting intensified as she settled on hard, muscular thighs. He tucked her head into his shoulder and stroked her hair while she cried. Just like every time before, the pain welled up and her sobs wracked her body. Her chest locked up. Panic set in and she began to hyperventilate.

"Claire!" Evan's voice was sharp and he smacked her firmly

on the thigh, which immediately redirected her from her panic. "Breathe." It was an order.

She took several deep, shuddering breaths between sobs to regulate her oxygen intake and let the pain flow through her. Memories flooded her. Her mother and father belittling her. Her sister ridiculing her. The reminders again and again that she was unwanted and unloved. The fact that the very people who were supposed to love her didn't want her.

Evan said nothing. He just held her as she cried, a solid, comforting presence. This was nothing like the beatings she'd provoked from Charlie. Those were violent and harsh and ended with recriminations and accusations. They'd go hours with her apologizing over and over and him berating her for pushing his buttons until he'd been forced to react. What Evan had done was controlled, intentional, and, in a very strange way, comforting.

Her voice was watery and barely above a whisper, but she forced the words out. "I feel worthless."

―⁓―

As her words sank into his marrow, he stroked the silk of her hair and just waited. It was all he could do. This was a necessary step. Introducing anything sexual without getting to the heart of her emotional pain was a recipe for disaster. As her dom, he'd be walking through a minefield in her psyche and she'd be vulnerable to a misstep by him every inch of the way.

She trembled so hard he wasn't sure how she even got the words out. Her tiny frame was featherlight in his lap. Her tears were wetting the shoulder of his T-shirt, but he didn't care. The sobs racking her body were gut-wrenching to hear. He was grateful that the erection he'd sprouted while spanking her had deflated in the face of her pain.

It had taken a supreme effort of will not to pull out his cock and bury himself inside her. Her creamy ass had been so tantalizing as it turned such a pretty shade of pink, the rosy lips of her sex exposed to his view. But the focus of this session hadn't been sexual, it had been emotional. Her walls were what held her back and they needed to get past them. That his own body had betrayed him seemed to be par for the course where Claire was concerned.

Now, though, as she talked of the emotional abuse she'd suffered, the feelings of loss and disconnection, and her shame and worthlessness, he just stroked her hair and rested his cheek against her head. He didn't join in or try to direct her words. Neither did he try to stop the tear that ran down his cheek as she poured out her pain to him.

He knew what path they needed to take now.

Chapter 12

CLAIRE SMOOTHED THE SILK of her dress over her hips and examined her reflection. She didn't recognize the woman in the mirror. The difference was subtle. It was the look in her eye, the set of her mouth, the tilt of her head. All were minutely different, and it was disorienting to feel almost like a stranger in her own skin.

Ever since the afternoon at Evan's apartment, she'd felt intrinsically altered. Loose and free-floating, like her pieces weren't quite anchored together anymore. She'd never told anyone the things she'd told Evan. Even Charlie, despite everything she'd pushed him to, had still only gotten the most superficial details. That she'd manipulated him into the beatings had put an intrinsic barrier on what she revealed.

Evan had been true to his word. He hadn't judged her, had only held her as she sobbed out all her fears and pain. When she was done, wrung out like a used sponge and a snotty mess in his lap, he'd sat her up, wiped her tears away with his thumbs, and said, "You are a beautiful, worthwhile, intelligent woman and it is time you learned that."

More tears had flowed at his words, but he'd not allowed those, telling her, "Tears are for things you can't change, not for things you can."

He'd sent her off to wash her face and then he'd taken her to dinner at Luna Bella where they'd talked more. She found she liked him very much. She'd been so hopelessly attracted to him for so long, she hadn't really evaluated him objectively. The more time they spent together, the more she saw the man underneath the broody façade he wore with her. He was extensively well read, an easy conversationalist, and they shared many of the same views on life and living; they even shared a love of classic movies and gourmet food. The only fly in the ointment was the reserve he maintained. He refused to talk any more about his wife and she sensed the key to Evan was his relationship with his wife.

They'd finished the evening with Evan escorting her home and accompanying her on her walk with Chester before leaving her with his instructions for their next meeting. She was to sign up for Chess Tutor online and learn the rules of chess. She was to play online for at least an hour each day. In addition, she was to begin a journal. Each day she was to write down any moments where she felt insecure or out of her element and how she resolved them or didn't. She was also to show up at his apartment wearing a dress with nothing underneath it two days later. When she'd questioned his instructions, his answer had been that she had to comply first and they would discuss them at their next meeting which, if she didn't get moving, she was going to be late for.

Grabbing her purse and keys, she hurried out the door. She walked the distance to Evan's apartment to give herself time to compose her nerves. The last few days had been confusing for her on many levels. The chess had been fun while still being a challenge. She'd learned the rules and some basic strategy, but she really disliked operating in the dark. She liked to know exactly what she was doing at any given time.

The journal was the hardest. She wasn't a writer. She was a reader. She didn't like sitting down to document her moments of weakness and insecurity. It forced her to replay a situation she already didn't like. The fact that she strongly suspected Evan was going to read it only made it worse. He'd instructed her to bring it with her and it currently burned a hole in her tote bag. Its weight seemed double that of the small, leather-bound book.

That she was naked underneath her dress was the most titillating. She'd had countless fantasies over the last few days of exactly what he would do to her. Even now, the image of him touching her or stroking her skin had her moistening. She shoved those thoughts away, though. Evan had told her no sex. No sense in getting all hot and bothered with no relief in sight. That depressing thought carried her up the steps to Evan's apartment.

———

Evan watched as Claire came down the street. She was dressed in a simple dress and he was guessing from the telltale jiggle of her breasts she was bare underneath as he'd directed her. His body very much liked that idea. His brain not so much, but he had plans for her today. Today was about breaking down her inhibitions while building up her image of herself. She had no idea how truly sensual she was. That she walked around with the notion that she was inadequate boggled his mind and made him want to find her parents and give them both a good kick in the ass.

He took a deep breath and willed his body into compliance before turning away from the window. A check of his preparations assured him everything was at the ready. The only thing missing was Claire. Before that thought even completed, she knocked on his door, setting his heart racing. *Fuck!* Where was his calm? Where was his composure? Why did this woman turn him upside down? Even in the early days with Marianne, he'd never been this nervous. He did not like this. No one bit.

With a deep breath, he willed his heart to slow down—not happening—and went to open the door. She barely filled the door-frame, but she loomed large in front of him. His personal torment in the flesh. Every single time, he couldn't decide whether to send her away or drag her into his arms. He did neither; instead, he moved aside and waved her in.

"How are you, Claire?" She had a pensive air about her. They'd need to discuss that first.

"I'm fine." She set her purse down on the counter and turned to face him, only to be distracted by the chess board set up on his small dinette. "We're playing chess?" She gave him a quizzical look. "Does this mean I get to finally find out why you are making me learn this game?"

He chuckled at her imperious look. "Yes, you do. But first, I'd like to know why you seem so"—he searched for the word—"reflective"—he quirked his head to the side and studied her—"thoughtful. Like you have something on your mind."

She raised an eyebrow. "You're very perceptive."

"I have to be in order to be a good dom."

"Why is that?"

"Well…" He waved her into a chair and she sat obediently while he leaned against the counter. "During scenes, there can be times where a sub is gagged or, for one reason or another, not fully present…"

"You mean subspace?" she interjected.

"Yes, there's that, but I also mean times where the sub might be distracted or just not fully aware of themselves for a number of reasons—stress, distraction, etc. It's my job to pay attention. To see the signs that indicate to me exactly where the sub is at and, if necessary, end the scene."

"Ah." She picked at the fabric of her skirt.

"For instance…" He stepped over, took her hand, and set it on the table before resuming his lean. "You pick at things when you're uncomfortable. Your clothes, your hair. That sort of thing." Her eyes went wide at that revelation. "So why don't you tell me why you are so uncomfortable right now."

For several very long moments, she just stared hard at him. The emotions crossing her face were fluid and mercurial. He didn't try to define them; he simply waited. Eventually, she dropped her gaze and murmured, "I really don't want you to read my journal."

"Why is that?"

"It seems too childish and whining."

"Elaborate, please."

She huffed an exasperated noise and gave him a peevish look, to which he said, "I'm not a mind reader, Claire. Perceptive isn't telepathic."

She laughed at that and her smile warmed his chest, causing a flare of anger that he ruthlessly shut down. Shaking her head ruefully, she said, "OK. OK. Look, I did what you asked, but when I reread it, it seems like I am making a big deal out of nothing or whining instead of getting to the heart of the matter." She shrugged before continuing, "It also makes me feel weak and I don't want you to see me that way." Her voice was barely above a whisper by the end and he felt his heart turn over at her vulnerability.

He came over to the table and took the chair catty-corner to hers. Taking her hand, he said, "Claire, I want you to listen to me very carefully. You are doing exactly what I wanted you to do… getting perspective. If you can reread what you wrote and see that there are times where you are reacting emotionally rather than rationally to the situation, then you have the opportunity to grow and rewrite your reactions the next time."

She squeezed his hand, and he returned the gentle pressure rather than doing what he wanted, which was to pull her into his lap and cuddle her; to wipe away that small frown of embarrassment that marred her expression while encouraging the pale pink flush that was spreading over her skin.

"As for me seeing you as weak, you are simply going to have to accept that if you feel that way, it's because *you* feel you are weak, and has nothing to do with me. I see you as a strong and capable woman who allows herself to be plagued by doubt. The purpose of the journal is for you to see yourself objectively and for us to discuss the situations that happened and then look at ways you can improve in the moment the next time. You, Claire"—he tapped her gently on the nose—"are your own worst enemy."

Tears were spilling down her cheeks. He reached out and collected them on a finger before rubbing them lightly over her soft lips. A mental groan rang through his brain as the unwanted image of his dick sliding through those lips, lubricated by her tears, sprang to mind, but he pulled himself back and said, "What did I tell you about tears, little one?"

"They are for things you can't change," came the watery reply.

"Can you change this?" His voice was soft.

"Yes," she whispered.

"Dry your eyes, little one." He released her hand and stood. "Time for you to put your chess skills to work."

"Huh?"

"I've been thinking on what you need, Claire. One of the things you allow yourself to be is plagued by doubt, but you don't take the time to both challenge and test yourself or to acquire skills for you to feel armed and ready to face the world and that, little one, is about to change."

At her incredulous look, he laughed out loud. "What, you thought dominance was all kinky sex?"

The flush of her skin deepened to an almost cherry red. His grin widened.

"Claire, the books often focus on the sex. It's arousing and sexual domination is awesome, but as a dom, and specifically as *your* dom, I am also responsible for helping you to attack the areas of vulnerability you allow to fester and undermine you."

He moved around to sit across from her and indicated the board. "Chess is a game of strategy with a long and illustrious history. To excel at chess is to learn how to think two and three steps ahead of your opponents. To see and read the battlefield and to be able to evaluate options, make determinations, then execute them. It is a game of skill and intellect, and one that is unparalleled throughout history. You, Claire, are going to have to beat me at chess. For each game you lose you get a punishment of my determination."

Her eyes flared wide and she gasped, "Like what?"

With a mischievous grin, he said in a deliberately offhanded tone, "Oh, I don't know, but I can be very, *very* creative."

He watched her squirm in her seat and noted how the pulse in her neck jumped. Inwardly, he groaned. He was going to have to be very careful.

<center>~~~</center>

"Checkmate." Evan's voice dripped over Claire like honey and sent a shiver down her spine.

Of course she'd lost. She was a novice and Evan, while no grand champion, was at least a competent player. He'd given her a bit of instruction as they went along. Before she placed each piece she was required to discuss her thinking. Sometimes he'd ask a question or two, but he never coached her. In the end, he'd still beaten her soundly.

"How many moves did I beat you in?" She'd been required to keep track.

"Ten."

"Very well, come with me."

He stood and walked toward the door at the far end of the living room. Obediently, she followed only to halt just inside the door when she realized she was in his bedroom. A large, king-size bed took up the majority of the room. A small door, for what was most likely a closet, was in the far corner and he'd built one of those modular open wardrobes along one wall that housed his clothing. He was meticulously neat and the unit looked like it could be featured in an advertisement for a closet organizing business. All of the clothes were separated by color and type and the hangers matched.

Claire experienced a pang of clothes envy looking at his setup. Her closet was not nearly as neat. The bed was covered in a dark, midnight blue coverlet over crisp white sheets and there were just two pillows on the bed. He clearly didn't waste time on extraneous niceties. But these things were not what had her halting.

No, it was the two freestanding, full-length mirrors next to the bed. One alongside it and the other at the foot. The bed was flanked on either side by sleek, wooden bed tables. The possibilities in front of her made her womb clench hard and her breath dissolved in her lungs.

"Come here, Claire." Evan stood next to the bed directly in front of one of the mirrors and indicated for her to join him.

She moved almost as if in a trance. She wasn't sure what to expect and did her best to calm her heart, which was currently running the Kentucky Derby in her rib cage. As she neared him, he took her hand and brought her to stand directly in front of him. Turning her by the shoulders, she faced the mirror. He loomed large behind her, at once a comfort and an intensely disturbing, sexual presence.

This was a scene she'd fantasized about many times. Evan placing her in front of the mirror and slowly undressing her before making love to her. Sadly, sex wasn't on the table, though clearly something was about to happen. Evan's hands lingered on her shoulders, massaging gently, his thumbs rubbing almost tenderly along her shoulder. Heat radiated from his body, warming her back, and she fought to remain still when she wanted badly to sink back into him.

"Open your eyes, Claire." Startled despite his soft tone, she met his gaze in the mirror. She hadn't even realized she'd closed them. "Undress for me, little one."

"I can't." The words were out before she even realized she'd spoken.

Evan's gaze was resolute as he said, "Do you remember your safe word?"

"Yes."

"What is it?"

"Red."

"Good. And when you are feeling extremely uncertain and close to the edge?"

"Yellow."

"You have only one choice tonight, Claire. You can do as I say, no questions asked until after, when we can and will discuss everything. Or you can use your safe word at any time to end the session. Understood?"

"Yes." She began to tremble at the knowledge that she was placing herself at Evan's mercy. Sure, she had the ultimate power in this situation. She could end it with a word, but would she be able to do this?

"Claire!" Evan's voice whipped out and her eyes snapped to his. "Pay attention, little one." She flushed, but nodded. "We discussed the rules of our sessions, did we not?"

"Yes."

"Have you broken any of those rules?"

"Yes."

"Which?"

"Questioning your instructions during a session instead of complying and waiting until after."

"That's right. Why do I require you to wait until after if you are capable of continuing?"

"Because you will push me to my limits, and what I consider my limits might not always be what you consider my limits."

"Exactly. If, for some reason, I take you somewhere you cannot bear, what is your recourse?"

"My safe word."

"Are you ready to use your safe word?"

"No."

"No, what?" His voice was like iron. Evan was gone, Sir had come in. But she didn't know Sir yet and that set her to trembling again.

"No, Sir." Her voice shook on the word and the connotation that went with it.

He ran his hands gently down her arms, raising goose bumps and setting her skin tingling, before gently squeezing her hands. He stepped away from her and sat on the edge of the bed where he could see her, but she could still see herself in the mirror.

"Undress for me, Claire. Remove each item one at a time. Fold it neatly and leave it on the end of the bed."

Paralyzed with embarrassment, Claire simply stood looking at herself in the mirror. She knew what was under these clothes and it wasn't a thin model-type. No airbrushed, perfect skin on her. No, she was a grown, almost middle-aged woman with all the flaws that went with that.

Evan said nothing, simply sat and waited, but the look of disappointment creeping into his features was enough to set her to fumbling with the hem of her dress. Her movements were jerky and she almost ripped the hem before yanking the garment over her head and holding it in front of her like a shield. She was so flat-chested, she really didn't want to stand bared before him. It was one thing when you were all caught up in the moment, kissing and pressed to each other. But there would be no hiding her diminutive stature from him this way.

Sneaking a glance at him, she saw that disappointed look growing. Just as he opened his mouth to speak, she took a deep breath, flicked the dress away from her, folded it, and set it on the bed. Evan merely nodded and gave her an encouraging smile. He said nothing. He didn't even look at her body; he only met her eyes and waited. For the briefest of moments, she fancied she saw a flare of heat there. All that lovely brown melting into deep, rich chocolate. In reality, the light was too dim and it was probably just wishful thinking anyway. A-cup breasts weren't usually what men craved.

Steeling herself, she stood stock-still and gave herself over to his scrutiny. That she was naked as the day she was born before Evan, the man who overtook her body and mind nightly in her fantasies, was so unbelievably surreal she began to feel almost as if she were a spectator on the scene rather than one of the main participants. That slight disconnection allowed her to feel calm as Evan began to look her over from head to toe.

His eyes lingered on her small breasts and rounded hips. She could see him catalogue her flaws, the cellulite adorning her thighs and ass. The imbalance of her body, with legs and hips slightly out of proportion with her petite upper body. Her mound, neatly trimmed, but nonetheless with puffy pink lips that were noticeable even when she wasn't aroused.

She waited for the disappointment and scorn. She waited for the words of disapproval that would be veiled as compliments. She waited for the hurt to start even as she wished he would touch her, lie to her and tell her she was beautiful. Maybe she could believe it this time. Maybe she would be able to forget herself for a few moments. Maybe—or maybe not.

Evan had moved to stand behind her and his face was set in harsh disapproval.

She took his breath away. When she'd arched to take the dress over her head, his every instinct had urged him to surge forward and suck her nipples into his mouth. To push that skirt up over her hips and ravish her pussy, which waited for him under that thin layer of fabric.

Her body was petite and she had breasts to match. Small, perfectly round mounds of silky flesh that were just begging to be licked, sucked, fondled, and tortured. Her nipples were large and puffy and tightening right before his eyes in the air conditioning. He wanted to reach out and squeeze them. Tug on them and watch them snap back.

She'd covered herself defensively. She was so insecure. It angered him. Who had made her feel so bad? As if her body was somehow inadequate. Her body was to be enjoyed and savored. He would tease out all her sensitive spots and help her understand that her body was as much an erotic playground as any voluptuous woman.

Just as he'd been about to admonish her for her delay, she'd continued, allowing him to watch the sway and jiggle of those tiny little tits as she folded her dress and set it down. Her hips were round and full, her ass sweetly curved and perfectly suited to being fondled and fucked. He was willing to bet money it was soft and her cheeks would hug and pillow his cock nicely. His body tightened viciously, but he didn't want to do anything to distract her. She had to be the one to undress. It was key that she choose to bare herself for him for this to work.

That she was frowning so fiercely at herself in the mirror was a problem. She was looking at herself as if someone had just betrayed her and left the knife in. That would not do at all.

It was time for the lessons to begin.

Standing, he moved to position himself behind her where they were both framed in the mirror. She refused to meet his eyes in the reflected image.

"What do you see?" he asked.

"Flaws." Her voice was flat and devoid of emotion. Definitely not good.

"I don't see any flaws." He kept his voice even.

"Then you aren't looking," she snapped.

Evan smacked her ass sharply. Not enough to bruise, but enough to sting. She yelped and began turning to face him, but he gripped her waist and kept her facing the mirror. Tears had flooded her eyes, but she was glaring. Better her angry than flat.

"Respect, little one. You've already earned two punishments today; are you going for three?" He made his voice firm even though part of him wanted to grin at her. Her fierceness was arousing. He was willing to bet she could be a tiger in bed if he could coax it out of her.

"No, Sir," she said, though it was more like growling since her teeth were clenched.

"What do you see?" He nodded again at the mirror. "And give the self-deprecation a rest. Talk to me."

"I see boobs that are way too small and an ass that is way too big. I see an imbalanced body and one that has too much fat and not enough muscle tone." The tears that had pooled in her eyes from the smack on her ass began tracking down her cheeks. "I see a body that can never compete with the big-breasted, fit, gorgeous women of the world, and I've been told so on many an occasion." Her voice was growing shrill. "I'm boyish, flat-chested, and unappealing. And I want to know why you are humiliating me this way—Sir?"

That last flabbergasted him. Humiliating her? That's what she thought this was. Oh no, no, no. She had much to learn. Stepping in close to her, he wrapped his arms around her waist and pulled her tight against him and, yes, she felt it...Those gorgeous eyes went wide. His erection pressed against her. Her ass was as soft as he'd imagined even through his jeans, and he wanted very much to bend her over and explore all that lovely flesh with his mouth, tongue, and fingers. Groaning, he steeled himself to refrain. No penetration. No sex. This was for Claire, not him. Marianne still had his heart, no matter how much his dick wanted Claire.

"Do you feel that, Claire?" His voice was hoarse as he fought to control his desires.

"Yes." Her voice was whisper soft.

"Does that feel like your body is unappealing?"

"Men have fucked me before, Sir." Hurt resonated in her voice so deeply it made his teeth itch. "So what? A man will get a hard-on easily enough."

"Not me." He waited for her eyes to meet his. Skepticism flooded her features, but he continued, "After Marianne died, no one made me hard. Only the memory of her, and I couldn't handle that. The pain was just too much." He let his hands rest on her waist; the soft, silky skin felt luscious under his fingers and his cock twitched. The flare in her eyes let him know she'd felt it. "After a while, it was like my body just went numb; sex was just no longer relevant. Then you walked into my shop and you—only you—made me hard. It was why I stayed away from you. Why you found me so unwelcoming. I'm still not ready for another relationship."

He stroked the skin of her hips and waist, allowing his cock to rest heavily against her ass so she could feel every surge and twitch.

"So, little one. How do you plan to refute that it was these small, little tits"—he cupped and lifted them gently, choking back the groan that threatened to escape—"and this full, round ass"—he rubbed his cock deliberately against her—"that made my body wake up? That was you, Claire. Not just any woman, *you*." He brought his hands back to her waist; otherwise he couldn't trust himself not to take her right then.

"I don't know," she said, her voice wavering.

"Stop trying then, and accept that you are very much appealing and enticing."

"I'll try, Sir."

"There is no try, only do," he said with a grin and she laughed as he'd hoped.

"I didn't know my dom was going to channel Yoda, Sir," she said on a giggle.

"Most versatile am I, little one." He grinned, continuing the joke and was pleased to see her relax. "Now, focus. What I want you to do is masturbate for me. Have you ever masturbated while someone watched?"

She'd gone rigid at his words, and only shook her head in response.

"Well, you're going to today. First, though, there's the issue of punishment for breaking the rules. Bend over, Claire."

The change in subject caught her off guard and he saw the confusion flash across her face, but she complied and the sight of her ass up in the air and her silky, pink pussy lips exposed before him were like a kick in the gut. He felt animalistic in his need to bury himself and own her.

Deep fucking breaths, Evan. Control yourself.

"What rule did you break, Claire?" He placed his hand on one cheek, stroking it lightly, enjoying the contrast between his own swarthy skin and her pale creaminess.

"I questioned you instead of complying after our session had already begun."

"That's right, little one. Questions are for after. You won't always understand what I'm asking you to do. Your safe word is your recourse if you feel I'm truly crossing your boundaries. Did you need your safe word?"

"No, Sir."

"Exactly. You were being rebellious and stubborn."

Smack. Evan spanked one perfectly round cheek and took inordinate pleasure in how the skin pinked nicely. Again and again he smacked her cheeks, loving the shake and jiggle and how red the skin was turning.

That pain was going to add to her orgasm, she just didn't know it yet. In between spanks, he rubbed and soothed the skin, murmuring to her how good she was being to accept her punishment. She was crying softly. Her tears flowed in a steady stream down her cheeks, and her body trembled under her restraint.

Unable to help himself, Evan reached between her legs and

palmed her pussy. She gasped. Her sex was drenched. Her juices coated his palm and the tops of her thighs.

"You like the pain, don't you?" He sank a finger into her pussy as he spoke, and she clenched around him.

"Yes…Sir." Her voice faltered as he added another finger and began to ply in and out of her core.

"That bothers you." It wasn't a question.

"Yes, Sir, it does," she whimpered when he added another finger to her hole. She was tight, almost viselike. The thought of how all that velvet heat would grip his cock had him on the verge of coming in his jeans.

"Why?"

"It's not normal, Sir." He heard her breath catch and wasn't sure if it was pain or his finger-fucking that brought the response on.

"Little one," he said gently as he pulled his fingers from her body and licked them despite himself. She was tangy and all female. Her taste was uniquely Claire and he wanted her desperately. *No!* Pull it together. He wiped his fingers on his jeans and said, "Normal is defined by a group, there is no intrinsic normal. Let it go. Pain is but the opposite of pleasure and they are symbiotic.

The body's natural response to pain is to create its own chemical pleasure. I use pain to enhance pleasure. Embrace it." He rubbed her ass again and noticed the slight wince; she'd be remembering that spanking for a while.

"Lie down, little one. You're not off the hook. It's time for you to masturbate for me."

She didn't want to do it, but her ass couldn't handle another spanking. She wasn't even sure she could get through it, but the look in Evan's eyes told her he was serious, and she wanted desperately to please him. To again see the approval that she'd never had before.

Carefully, she settled herself on his bed and luxuriated for a moment in the soft silkiness and the musky scent that drifted across her from his sheets. The fire on her ass was radiating out across her skin and fading into a pleasant pins and needles feeling that she found she quite enjoyed. Rather than sexual, she felt embarrassed and self-conscious.

Evan settled himself at the end of the bed where he had a bird's-eye view of her hoo-ha if he just leaned forward a bit and she froze. She couldn't do it. She couldn't sit here and masturbate in front of him. She'd fantasized endlessly about this by this point. And never in all those fantasies did she feel so unattractive and ugly and completely lacking as she did in this moment. She didn't even truly understand what was going on or what his purpose was.

Tears burned her eyes and she squeezed them shut. She could feel the hot streaks burrowing down her cheeks and dripping into her ear.

"Talk to me, little one." His voice was gentle but firm.

"I can't." She choked out the words.

"Can't talk to me or can't masturbate?"

She sniffled and rubbed her nose. "Both." She knew she sounded pathetic.

"Why?"

"I'm embarrassed."

"Why?"

"Because I don't feel sexy at all. I feel stupid." She didn't like the whine that was creeping into her voice.

"Are you going to let that stop you?"

Not the answer she'd been expecting and she had no response to that.

"If you're embarrassed," he continued, "it's because you're choosing to be." He said nothing more.

She searched his face, but there was nothing more to see there; it was impassive. At least there was no pity in his gaze.

Closing her eyes, she took a deep breath and hesitantly brought her hands to her breasts. Her hands were tiny and the soft mounds filled her palms, though she doubted they'd do the same in Evan's hands. No, his would be large and warm and cup them fully. Going with that thought, Claire blocked out everything else and embraced the fantasy. She massaged her breasts and began to squeeze and roll her nipples, imagining they were Evan's hands instead of her own. Her nipples tightened and she continued to pull and tug them, taking pleasure in the slight zings of sensation that shot down into her swelling clitoris.

She imagined Evan getting up and moving to lean over her, kissing and sucking on her nipples, and she felt her clitoris pulse in response. Slowly, she stroked down her body. Her lips were puffy and slick. She danced her fingers over her tightly trimmed curls, feeling her moisture with her fingertips. She dipped into her folds and danced her fingers across her clitoris. She arched and moaned, imagining Evan's touch instead of her own.

On impulse she brought her fingers to her mouth and sucked her moisture off them, something she'd never done before. A deep, long groan brought her out of her fantasy and she opened her eyes to see Evan looking at her as if she were a nice big steak and he was a hungry animal. His eyes burned and his hand moved along his cock, which he'd obviously taken out at some point. He looked ravenous, and she bloomed under the knowledge that she had such an effect on him.

She watched his big hand stroke his cock rhythmically and she matched that rhythm in her own pussy. She dipped her fingers in and out, feeling her intimate muscles contract around her fingers before pulling out and rubbing her clitoris. Evan's eyes were riveted to where she worked her pussy, and she grew even bolder. Calling up various things she'd read in all those stories, she smacked her pussy hard, gasping at the unexpected pleasure that shot through her body.

She glanced at Evan's face. It was dark and furious yet somehow not scary in any way. He looked almost tortured, but his cock was throbbing and pulsing in his hands and she could see the bead of moisture forming at the tip. She wanted desperately to lick it off but was scared that if she did anything like that, she'd not only kill the mood, but would also cause him to end their agreement altogether.

Instead, she contented herself with imagining that she did it and licked her lips at the thought, eliciting a growl from Evan that set her blood on fire. She was alternating between slapping her clit and rubbing it furiously as the tension built.

"Come for me, little one." Evan's voice was deep and barely intelligible.

She reached for one of her nipples, squeezing and rolling it hard as she rubbed her clitoris. The fire slowly radiated out through her limbs; her nipples went rigid, and every muscle clenched as her orgasm swamped her. She pressed down hard, forcing each sensation to linger as she rode the wave of her orgasm. Her cries were unintelligible as she bucked and writhed under Evan's searing gaze.

Just as she began to come back to herself, Evan surged toward her, demanding, "Open your mouth."

She complied as he planted a knee on the bed and stroked his cock, which jutted out proud and firm from his body. His balls were drawn up tight and he was fully engorged. It didn't take long before he growled again and pressed the head of his cock to her lower lip, forcing her mouth wide to take in his full girth. He pressed his cockhead between her lips and jet after jet of hot, thick semen flooded her mouth. She gulped and sucked at him greedily, but he kept back, not going any deeper.

As he pulled back, she smiled up at him, thrilled that he'd joined in, only to see the furious look on his face. All joy died in that moment.

She was sublime in her orgasm and it absolutely killed him. He hadn't been able to help himself. Not when she'd given in to herself and begun to masturbate without reserve, not when she'd noticed him working his cock over like it owed him money and she'd grown so bold, and not when she'd finally come. He'd had to mark her, claim her in some way.

The sight of her full, sexy lips engulfing the head of his cock was pure torture. He wanted to own her mouth, to fuck it hard and then pull out and slam himself into her pussy, marking her fully. But she wasn't his and she wasn't going to be. He wasn't going there. He never wanted to go through what he went through—

All thought left his brain as he absorbed the crushed look on Claire's face. He quickly stuffed his cock back into his jeans and sat on the bed, taking her hand.

"Talk to me, Claire." He heard the urgent concern in his voice and sought to calm down. Tears welled in her eyes and he stroked the hair back from her forehead.

Her voice was small and watery and she wouldn't look at him as she said, "You look angry."

He could have kicked his own ass in that moment. The last thing she needed was to think that she'd displeased him in any way. Stretching out next to her, he gathered her into his arms. She was rigid and unyielding and lay like a 2x4 against him.

"Relax, Claire." His voice was firm and he waited until she complied, her petite shape molding itself to his much larger one. He held her there, petting her hair gently, trying to find the right words to convey what had just happened without making it any worse, and was at a loss. "You were…" He wanted the right word and went with honest in the end. "Sublime."

She went still.

"Claire, you were amazing to watch, sexy and uninhibited. You see you had a serious effect on me."

"But why did you look so angry?" Her voice was still soft, but there was an edge of backbone back. She didn't sound lost.

"Because you tempt me in ways I'm not prepared to deal with, little one." The truth spilled out despite himself. "I don't want to rehash this again and again, but this is not about sex, and you tempt me too much for my own good." He dropped a light kiss on her forehead.

She felt very good lying there next to him. Too good. He shifted and put a bit of space between them even as he knew himself for an asshole. He needed to handle her aftercare appropriately. He relaxed and gathered her close, took a deep breath, and continued.

"Do you know why I had you do that just now?"

She shook her head.

"Because you need to see yourself the way I do. Sensual, beautiful, erotic." She went still as he spoke, but he didn't look at her. "You captivated me, Claire, and yet you are so ridiculously critical of yourself it makes my teeth itch. I'd spank it right out of you if I thought I could accomplish that. Instead, I do this so you can learn to see yourself differently."

Beside him, she was silent. A quick look showed him that she'd fallen asleep. Without the pressure of discovery, Evan looked his fill. Her beauty was a quiet kind. She wouldn't turn heads on the street, but it was there nonetheless. For him at least, it was seared into his brain.

In the aftermath of their session, her eyes were just a bit puffy and the telltale tracks of her tears were visible on her cheeks. Her lips were soft and lush and the image of his cock between them zinged through his mind. Her body was soft and pliant in his arms, and so utterly delectable he wanted to consume her. Being careful not to wake her, he gently pressed his lips over one of the trails from her tears and lingered, touching his tongue to the salty line, tasting her skin and inhaling her soft scent. His cock was stirring and he had to get out of there or he was going to do something he wouldn't be able to come back from.

Gently, he disengaged himself from her and settled in his bed, covering her with the duvet. Turning off the light, he left her there.

Chapter 13

Woohoo! CLAIRE CLOSED THE window of the online chess game she had just won with a grin on her face, pushed back from her desk, and went to change her clothes. Ten rounds. That was her "punishment" from Evan for losing to him. She had to play ten rounds before their next session, which wasn't for a few days, but she'd wanted to get them out of the way. She'd won three of the ten rounds including this one, but that was three more than she'd won before. It might not translate to beating Evan yet, but she was definitely improving.

Checking her watch, she saw it was time to get ready to meet Bridget. She headed into her room and pulled out a pair of slim, white capris and a ruby-red tank top, sliding them over her body and slipping on some high-wedged sandals. She checked herself out in the mirror. She looked different. She couldn't really pinpoint it, but it was there. She felt more... whole. The lines and tiredness were fading from her face.

Admittedly, her exploration with Evan was forcing her to examine areas of herself and her psyche in ways she hadn't even considered when they'd agreed he would be her dom. She hadn't thought of anything outside the bedroom, or the manner in which he would creatively find ways to challenge her ingrained thoughts and feelings. Having her masturbate for him had been a serious breakthrough for her. Until now, she'd barely been able to masturbate for herself; to do it for him had been mind-altering. Add in the fact that she'd been instructed to masturbate in front of the mirror throughout the week and to use a vibrator in the process and she'd learned more about her body in the last few days than in the entire time she'd been having sex.

Waking up in Evan's bed had been bittersweet because she'd been alone, but it had smelled like them both and she'd luxuriated for a few minutes, taking in the whole experience. She'd risen, dressed, and gone out to see Evan, who'd been on the couch watching golf. Their parting had not been quite what she'd hoped for after what they'd shared. He'd been polite, exceedingly polite, but not warm.

With a sigh, she shook her head to clear out the self-pity wanting to take root. She'd known when she'd agreed to be his sub that romance wasn't on the table. Finding her smile, she grabbed her keys and Chester and headed out the door.

She arrived at Bean There Done That before Bridget did and secured a table for them on the patio. She tied Chester up and gave him his chew toy as she gave the barista her order for a cappuccino. She sipped the silky brew and pondered whether she should even bring up her concerns to Bridget about what the real problem was for Evan. It wasn't so much that she felt he needed to want to have sex with *her* per se. It was more that she felt any relationship, especially one as intimate as hers was growing with Evan, should be symbiotic and synergistic. They should be helping each other grow and Evan had thrown a wall up.

It didn't seem healthy, and, frankly, she felt a seed of doubt in her newfound confidence every time she thought about it. That he found her attractive was not in question. His response to her during their session had been sincere, she was sure of that, but...*Sigh*... That was exactly the problem, the "but." When he'd come in her mouth it had been amazing to watch him. His eyes had been closed and the pleasure on his face had been unbelievable. That she'd been responsible for such rapture had been transcendent. She'd never felt sexier and more confident in herself as an attractive woman as she had at that moment. So his withdrawal after had cut.

Even as that thought crossed her mind, her confidence tried to falter once again, but she would be damned if she was going to allow what had happened with Charlie to befall her again. Her self-worth was not going to be determined by any man, not even one she'd fallen in love with.

The thought hit Claire with the impact of a semitruck and she was glad she was sitting down. She wasn't sure that she wouldn't have fallen over if she hadn't been. Love was so not in the plans here. Infatuation, sure, but love would just screw everything up. She didn't want to be in love with Evan. Not when the man was so closed off.

Karma was a bitch, wasn't it? She'd been completely closed off to Charlie and now here she was, completely ass over elbow for a man who didn't want her in that way. She stared blankly out across the street at the people walking by as the feeling of despondency washed over her. This was so not the way she wanted this to be.

"Hey there, darlin'." Bridget's sultry drawl pulled her out of her morose thoughts. "What's got you glaring at passersby?"

Bridget looked phenomenal as usual. Her coppery hair was piled on top of her head and dropping all around in ringlets that somehow looked regal on her tiny frame rather than doll-like as it would have on so many others.

She sat across from Claire and set what smelled like a chai tea down on the table. In her customary fashion, she reached into her handbag of magic tricks, as Claire liked to think of it since she seemed to always have whatever the situation required in its depths, and handed Chester a dog biscuit. For his part, Chester gently took the cookie and nuzzled her hand.

Claire snorted inelegantly. "You're spoiling him, ya know.

Now he'll only eat those ridiculously expensive gourmet biscuits you get him."

Bridget arched an eyebrow, saying, "If you wouldn't eat it, now why should he, sugar?" even as she scratched him behind the ears and baby talked him.

Claire just snorted again, earning a sharp look from Bridget, who inquired, "Are you going to tell me what's going on or are we going to play ten questions?"

"Twenty questions," Claire fired back even as she knew she was being snotty with Bridget, who didn't deserve to catch backlash from her discomfort over her revelation.

"Ten questions, darlin'." She grinned. "I don't feel up to twenty, and besides, I think I already know what is the cause of the problem, if not the details, so why don't you spare your aging friend the trouble and just spill it?"

"Hardly aging, Bridg," she huffed, but took a deep sigh and said, "It's Evan."

"Um-hmm," Bridget murmured. "You finally figured out you're in love with him?"

"How on earth did you know that?" Claire was astounded. She'd only just figured it out herself.

Bridget laughed out loud, drawing the attention of the elderly couple at a nearby table before she covered her mouth and giggled at Claire's obvious disbelief.

"You haven't seen how you look when he's nearby or the way your face changes when you talk about him. Or how you've been glowing all week ever since your date—"

"It wasn't a date," Claire interjected.

"Whatever." Bridget waved her words off as if they were of no more import than air.

"Seriously," Claire said, feeling the need to push the point. "It wasn't a date."

"OK," Bridget said, but it was in that tone that made it clear she was just humoring Claire.

"I. Mean. It." Claire's words were clipped and underscored as she felt her anger grow.

Bridget looked up, startled at the tone of Claire's words, and set down the chai tea that had been on its way to her lightly glossed lips. "Talk to me, honey. What's he done?"

Claire deflated at the obvious concern in Bridget's voice and tears welled in her eyes, spilling down her cheeks. Alarm flashed across Bridget's face. She came around to Claire's side of the table and sat next to her, putting an arm across her shoulders and hugging her tight.

Claire laid her head on Bridget's shoulder and just let herself sob quietly for a few minutes before finally pulling herself together. She excused herself briefly and went to the ladies' room to wash her face before coming back to the table. Her stomach turned over, knowing she was going to have to talk to Bridget about this now. One didn't cry all over one's best friend and not provide an explanation.

Bridget followed her with worried eyes as she made her way back to the table. She'd retaken her original seat and was sipping her tea.

"He doesn't want me and I'm in love with him," Claire blurted before her butt even touched the seat. "And I just freakin' figured it out right now."

"That he doesn't want you or that you're in love?"

For the life of her, Claire didn't know why that struck her as funny, or maybe she was just going into hysterics, but she laughed at the matter-of-fact way Bridget restated her own words and replied with a grin, "That I'm in love. He'd made it clear that romance wasn't in the cards for us before."

"Bull butter!" Bridget gave a very unladylike snort and the outrageous words had Claire laughing all over again.

"What in the hell is bull butter?"

Bridget grinned at her and replied with a smug look, "Daddy didn't allow us to curse growing up, so I made up words to substitute for the expletives. He couldn't punish me if I wasn't cursing even though we both knew what I meant. So if it will help you, my slow-on-the-uptake friend—bullshit. Evan very much wants you."

Claire shook her head in negation and Bridget nodded her head in affirmation, saying, "We can go back and forth all day, but that man absolutely wants you. You didn't see the snarling, spitting bear he became when you left the club and refused to come back to the shop. Since you and he have been having your 'sessions'"—Bridget threw up the air quotes—"he's been prancing around like the cat that got the canary."

"I dunno," Claire said to buy time to gather her thoughts. "After we…" She waved her hand in the air as she searched for the right word and was relieved when Bridget nodded her understanding. "I fell asleep and when I woke up, I was alone. I went out to see him and say good-bye and he was so polite."

"Isn't polite usually a good thing?" Bridget's smile was a mix of tender and teasing.

"Yes, but not when it is rigidly polite. You know what I mean. Everything is just so and there is no informality at all." She huffed a frustrated breath. "It's like we were strangers."

"Really?" Bridget looked stunned. "Did you two…?" She trailed off, her peaches and cream skin turning a shade of pink that was so sweet Claire almost chuckled.

"No, not that. We didn't have sex." Claire was stunned at her own bluntness, but hell, how could she have this conversation if she beat around the bush? She dropped her voice to a whisper. "He came in my mouth, but we didn't have sex." And she really did laugh this time at Bridget's obvious discomfort.

Pulling herself together, she said, "I'm sorry, Bridg. I just don't know any way to have this conversation other than straight up."

Bridget grinned and said, "It's my Southern sensibility, honey. Don't you know that any Southern belle worth her salt just lies back and thinks of England? We don't enjoy sex." She smirked and laughed too.

The shared humor made it easier for Claire to get the words out. "He told me from the beginning that sex and romance of any kind were out of the question. And I agreed to it, but here I am in love with him and he's not in love with me. I'm violating our agreement."

"Did you agree not to have feelings for him?"

"No, but—"

"Did you agree to not having sex with him?"

"Yes, but—"

"It sounds to me like you are keeping your agreement."

"Yes, but—" Claire paused this time, expecting to be cut off. "He is still in love with Marianne."

"No, he's not." Bridget's words were steely and brooked no argument.

"What do you mean?" Claire was taken aback by her certainty.

"There's something else there. I'm certain of it. Not sure what it is, though, darlin'. But it ain't still being *in love* with Marianne."

She sipped her chai before continuing.

"Honey, he's always going to love Mari, you know that, but when she first died, and for the last several years, it's been as if other women didn't exist. He was a shell of himself. He went through life performing the expected motions. I saw him start to wake up when you first came around, and since the two of you entered into your little arrangement, he reminds me of when Mari was still here—alive."

"But—" She held up her hand to stave Claire off.

"Now, let me finish, darlin', and then you can 'but' me to your heart's content." She took a final sip of her tea. "You, m'dear, are the reason for that change. I'm not going to declare his heart to you—only he can say whether he loves you or not—but I can tell you he's definitely *not* still pining away for Mari. Whatever is going on, it's something other than that."

Claire was absolutely stupefied. "Well, hell, Bridg. What do I do, then?"

Bridget grinned and said, "Well, I guess you talk to him, honey. Preferably before he sticks his dick in your mouth and you can't get a word out."

Claire was so shocked at Bridget's explicitness that she damn near snorted her cappuccino, much to Bridget's delight.

Evan watched the women laughing from his SUV while he waited to turn down Main Street. They didn't see him, and they appeared quite happily ensconced in whatever conversation they were having.

Seeing Claire so freely happy moved him deeply. His heart squeezed, and he'd found himself grinning just because she was smiling so delightedly. He wondered what they were talking about, and almost parked so he could go join them and be near her. That would not do.

Their time together was not going as planned. He had thought to get rid of this compulsion to take care of her by ensuring her introduction to BDSM went smoothly. All those protective instincts would settle down then.

Yeah. Right.

He was anything but settled. He still dreamed of her. She still dominated his waking thoughts and fantasies. Even more so now he'd seen her in the flesh, so wanton and willing.

He'd lost control. He'd simply been unable to resist her in the moment, and seeing those full lips wrapped around his cock had been, literally, a dream come true.

He'd been distant with her when she'd woken and he'd seen the hurt in her face. He reminded himself that he'd never lied to her. He'd told her there was no possibility of a relationship between them other than dom and sub. That he was still in love with his wife.

If he'd been so fucking honest with her, why did he feel like he was lying? Why did he feel like he owed her an apology?

The blare of a horn interrupted Evan's thoughts and he saw that he was sitting through the turn signal. Stepping on the gas, he turned the corner, but unfortunately clarity didn't come with him.

Chapter 14

"DAMN IT!" CLAIRE COULDN'T hide her frustration. She'd been so close to beating Evan this time. She'd lost soundly the first two games, but this time she'd been very close. She had been practicing quite regularly and was winning more of her matches online, but she hadn't won a round with Evan yet. And this game was long. She'd stopped counting at twenty moves as she worked every angle she could think of to beat him.

Evan smiled at her but only shook his head, not looking at her while he placed the pieces back in the case. "You've gotten much better since the last time we played. You must be practicing a lot."

"Yeah, I have, actually. I've been playing every evening after I walk Chester." She helped remove the pieces from the board and folded it, handing it to Evan to be placed back in the box.

"What about your journal? Have you been keeping up with that?"

"Yes." She took the box from him and placed it on the bookshelf where it belonged. "But I find I'm writing less simply because I have fewer troubling incidents to write about. I'm feeling more confident and I'm asserting myself more, so I'm less hostile and out of sorts."

She still wasn't completely comfortable moving around Evan's house. It was like there was a specter that hovered nearby. A shadow haunting Evan. Nothing Freudian there or anything. She felt Marianne's presence between them, even though they never discussed it. She was getting to the point that she wasn't sure who was doing the haunting.

She'd been unsuccessful in bringing the topic up to Evan both because some part of her felt as if she were violating their agreement if she did, but also because she wasn't quite ready to hear that she wasn't what he wanted or needed and how he preferred to love a ghost than a real live woman.

Turning away from the bookshelf, she stopped short at the sight of a flogger in Evan's hands. He had a small wooden chest out on the table and was removing several implements from it and laying them out on the table.

Slowly, she moved to his side and watched as he laid out a suede flogger. It was beautiful to look at, and instinctively she reached out to run her fingers over it, only to stop and hover just above it, not at all sure if she should touch it without permission or not.

Seeing her hesitation, Evan said, "Go ahead, it's OK. I bought it for you."

"You did?"

A look of pain flashed across his face as he nodded and said in a slightly rough voice, "Yes, you deserved new toys, just for you."

Claire looked down and stroked the fine leather of the flogger. She felt a wealth of unspoken emotion in that response and a small seed of anger took root in her heart. She wanted to reach in and pluck it out, but couldn't when a simple gesture that should have been sweet was being tarnished by a ghost she couldn't compete with.

Squeezing her eyes tight, she took a deep breath, found her smile, and said, "Thank you, Sir. I appreciate that."

Evan's hand flexed convulsively around the vibrator he'd just pulled out of the box and she could have sworn she heard him suck in a breath. A small feeling of triumph passed through her. It was childish, she knew, but he affected her so deeply yet held himself so remotely, torturing them both with the ghost of his dead wife and sub.

They'd met regularly over the week for coffee and to talk. They were getting to know each other and she was quite gratified to find Evan talking with her more about his background and his past. With one glaring exception. Marianne. He refused to discuss her, other than to say she'd died from ovarian cancer. His lips were sealed tighter than Fort Knox and she was tired of trying to pry the information out of him.

Again and again, she reminded herself that they were not dating, and she was his sub, not his lover, to the point it was almost a ritualistic chant in her mind.

He set the vibrator down on the table and pulled out an anal plug along with a bottle of lube. The implications of the toys on the table stole her breath and made her pussy swell. She felt the moisture flood her core and knew her nipples were hard. Her chest constricted, and she had to willfully calm her now racing heart. She'd wanted this since *Finding Herself* and now that it was here, she was going into overdrive.

"Claire." He tipped her chin up. "Relax, baby girl. I'm going to take care of you." He searched her face. His own was unreadable. "Do you trust me?"

She nodded since her voice seemed to have dissolved.

"Good." He released his hold on her chin. "Go into the bedroom and strip. Lie on your stomach on the bed and wait for me there."

"Yes, Sir." She looked away as she spoke and didn't notice the hunger with which Evan looked at her as she hurried to obey.

Evan simply stared. Claire had done exactly as he'd asked and was lying naked across his bed. Her creamy skin glowed against the midnight of his coverlet, and the swell of her ass was ripe for what he planned.

He brought the toys he'd removed from the toy box and set them on the table next to his bed. She turned her head and watched, but said nothing. All of these were untouched, purchased especially for her. Everything he'd owned before, he'd trashed after Marianne had died. He couldn't bear to look at them.

Moving to stand beside the bed, he bent and began to simply stroke and caress Claire's skin, allowing himself to luxuriate in its silken texture. The fine hairs along her skin rose up almost as if reaching out for him, and he felt his cock begin to stir. He wanted very badly to make love to her, but he wasn't going to go there. Period.

He refused to examine his resistance. It was simply going to be as he decided. That was all that mattered to him. That he be in control this time. His hands stopped their motion on that thought, but he journeyed no further down that path as Claire flexed and sighed on the bed, distracting him.

He glanced at her face. Her eyes were closed and she looked incredibly relaxed. Peaceful almost. His cock twitched and he adjusted himself to relieve the pressure. Resuming his massage, he watched in fascination as her skin rippled and danced under his fingers. It was as if her body were an instrument and he was tuning it.

This was a new experience for him and he wasn't sure how to react to that knowledge. He and Marianne had clicked so completely, but he couldn't remember a moment like this. He'd known her intimately, played her like she was a violin and he a maestro, but he couldn't recall her body responding so viscerally to a simple touch.

The flex and sway of Claire's body was hypnotic. A silent siren's call. He felt the pull to touch her deeper, harder, and with more force. It was almost compulsive. With an effort of will, he pulled himself back and straightened. Turning, he busied himself with the plug and lube to collect his thoughts and calm his mind.

He sat next to Claire on the bed. She tensed briefly but relaxed again when he continued to stroke her ass and lower back. He was enjoying the simple feel of her ass under his hand so much he was almost reluctant to move forward. This basic connection with her was peaceful, but peaceful wasn't what he was going for. Today, he wanted to push her boundaries and show her that pain was the perfect counterpoint to pleasure.

———∿∿∿———

Claire held herself perfectly still. She didn't want to take any chance of disturbing the moment. Evan's hand was stroking light circles on the cheeks of her ass and it was taking a supreme effort to refrain from pressing into his hand and silently begging for more. There was an odd vibe in the room, though; something tickling the back of her mind, telling her to remain still, that any movement would disturb this peace.

She felt intrinsically linked to him in this moment. Her cells felt as if they were straining toward him. Even her mind felt like it was reaching for him, and she was incredibly aroused just from a simple massage. It went without saying that she'd never experienced anything like this. Her nipples were hard points, and her pussy was dripping.

She couldn't contain her shudder as she felt his finger trail through her slit and then stroke her moisture along the rosebud of her anus. She clenched at the unfamiliar touch but relaxed as Evan gave her a moment to adjust. He stroked her anus, dipping minutely in, not truly penetrating, teasing more than anything. To her surprise, her arousal spiked even higher as he toyed with her and, without her truly being conscious of it, she began to flex and strain toward him so that she was forcing his finger deeper with each pass.

Her womb clenched. She began to feel empty and in need of filling. It was shocking to her; her ass shouldn't be so tightly related to her pussy, but heaven help her, she wanted to be fucked hard—in both holes. Goose bumps erupted on her skin and she was actively flexing and pressing into Evan's finger. He gently pulled back, and she almost whimpered at the cessation of such a lovely feeling.

She jumped a bit when a cool liquid ran along her cleft and she realized it was lube. She kept her eyes closed and willfully forced herself to relax. Anal sex had always been a torture test for her. Charlie had demanded it and she'd acquiesced out of guilt, but she'd never enjoyed it. It had hurt. Every single time. But then, she'd never been able to convince Charlie to use lube either. He didn't like the way it felt or smelled. He had a thousand reasons for why he didn't use it that all came down to pain for her.

Evan rubbed the lube around her pucker, then dipped inside. His finger slid into her easily and she gasped at this new sensation. Pulling out, he added another finger to the mix, slowly stretching her. He fucked her ass gently, allowing her to adjust, and soon she was moaning and straining back against his hand.

It was unlike anything she'd expected. It didn't hurt and it didn't feel pleasurable per se, but he was doing crazy things to her clitoris which you could have knocked her over with a feather to realize. Each thrust into her ass had the underside of her clitoris zinging and she clenched the sheets in response. Instinctively, she was grinding into the mattress with each counterthrust against Evan's fingers.

Smack! She jumped as Evan slapped her ass cheek.

"Be still." His voice was hoarse and gruff. She could barely make out the words, but she relaxed and did her best to lie still. "Have you ever had a plug inside you, Claire?"

"No, Sir."

"You've had anal sex, though?"

"Yes." There must have been something in her tone because Evan stilled, much to her disappointment.

"You don't like anal sex?"

"It's hard to like something that hurts so badly, Sir." A cock in her ass might hurt, but his fingers were feeling pretty damn good and she wanted more of that.

"Sometimes pain is part of the experience, but it should never be so painful that you can't enjoy it and, frankly, it is possible to have anal sex with no pain at all."

She couldn't help herself; she snorted derisively.

"Do you disbelieve me?"

"Let's just say I'm skeptical, but I expected that when I signed up for this with you there would be some pain involved." Belatedly, she remembered to add, "Sir."

"You weren't with the right partner, little one. Anal sex is about trust. Yes, there is domination and yes, there is sometimes pain, but what it really is about is trusting your partner with something so forbidden. Trusting him to take care of you and ensure your pleasure even in such an intimate act."

The tone of Evan's voice had altered and she couldn't quite figure out what it was, but he resumed his steady penetration of her ass, this time scissoring his fingers a bit as he pressed deeply into her back passage. She moaned as the zings in her clitoris returned.

Slowly, he withdrew his fingers. She felt him rub more lube into her pucker, then a blunt pressure against her anus, and she tensed.

"No, little one." He used his other hand to rub gently on her lower back. "Take a deep breath for me, blow it out and relax. Then I want you to push out as I insert this."

"But—" She trailed off.

Questioning him was not the thing to do in this moment. Instead, she did her best to comply. Taking a deep breath, she consciously relaxed her muscles and pressed out against the plug. She felt herself stretching, felt the ring of muscle pull and tighten just to the point of pain, but never crossing it. Evan maintained a gentle, even pressure and soon she felt the plug pop into place past the tight ring of muscle.

It didn't hurt. It didn't quite feel good, but it didn't hurt. She felt full and stretched and surprisingly aroused. Her nipples were hard berries poking her, and she had the strong desire to have them squeezed and tugged. Her pussy was soaking, and she desperately wanted Evan's cock. She was a mass of sensation and need and all he'd done was plug her ass.

She fought the desire to writhe on the bed, to reach between her legs and soothe the ache that was growing there.

"How is that, little one?"

"Fine, Sir."

"Tell me what you're feeling." It wasn't a request.

She could feel herself blushing, but she said, "I feel full and stretched and my clit is pulsing. My nipples ache and I want to grind myself into the bed to relieve pressure. I want to move."

She heard him chuckle at the plaintive note in her voice that couldn't be missed.

"Does it hurt?" His voice was soft.

"No, Sir." It didn't hurt; it was stimulating in a way she'd never experienced. It *definitely* didn't hurt.

"I'm going to flog you, Claire."

The words raced across her skin like fire. She'd read about flogging. Envisioned it many times in her mind, but had no idea what it would be like. She was afraid and intrigued and downright ravenous all at once.

"It's time you learned to channel your need for pain."

As he spoke, she felt him stand, and she opened her eyes. He lifted up the flogger from the side table. It was beautiful in its own right. The grip was big enough to fit Evan's hand comfortably, and the ebony surface shone as if it were coated with lacquer. The strands appeared almost suedelike where they swung in the light. She shivered with uncertainty at what was about to happen, but, like Evan said, this was about trust, and trust him she would.

Evan's cock was about to explode. As he'd fingered her ass, it had been his cock he'd wanted to shove in there, not a damn plug. He was now stroking her skin with the flogger, waking it up, so to speak. She lay still, trembling slightly, and he was desperate to fuck her. Part of him wanted to send her packing and never see her again. He'd sworn he wasn't going to fuck her, sworn this wasn't about sex, but damn it, all he could think about was getting inside her.

The flogger was soft, designed to sting more than truly hurt, and it would pink up her skin nicely. He lashed her ass lightly and everything in him clenched right along with her as she moaned and squeezed her ass against the sting. He wasn't hitting her hard; if anything, it should be creating a light stinging sensation rather than any real pain. Marianne had once said that gentle flogging wasn't that different than the resulting sting of having her eyebrows waxed.

He began to set up a rhythm alternating sides along Claire's body. Spreading the sting out so that her entire ass and lower back would be covered in sensation. Her lush, creamy skin was streaked with light pink lines and she was trembling and writhing on his bed, moaning with each strike.

He set the flogger down and reached between her legs while asking, "How are you doing, little one?" His answer was in the flood of juice from her pussy, but he wanted to ensure she was still with him.

"Good, Sir." Her voice was barely a whisper and her breathing was harsh.

"Can you handle more?" He thrust his fingers into her pussy as he spoke and she groaned loudly, clenching around his fingers. He pulled out and added a third finger, fucking her vigorously as she humped his hand.

"Yes, Sir," she moaned and gripped the coverlet with two fists, lifting her ass in the air and inviting more from him.

Evan pulled his fingers out and reached for the flogger. He couldn't resist, though, and he licked her juice from his fingers. She was tangy and sweet and that taste just wet his appetite for more of her delectable pussy. His mouth literally watered in the need to lap all that lovely honey from her cunt. Next time, he was going to shave her bare. All the better for her to feel every little sensation he gave her. Which gave him an idea. With the way she was responding, he was almost certain she'd enjoy what he had in mind.

"Roll over, baby girl."

She complied, rolling onto her back. The plug was still inside her, and she winced briefly when her ass made contact with the bed. Evan repeated the process from before, stroking her skin lightly with the flogger.

"Spread your legs, baby. Show me your pussy."

Her legs opened and her pussy glistened in the soft light of his bedroom. Her plump lips were deep red and pouty, just begging to be sucked and licked and flogged. He struck lightly, but she moaned loudly and gripped the sheets, arching hard. Her small, round tits thrust up into the air.

Evan heard the involuntary moan that could only have come from him at the carnal sight she made. Her eyes were closed and sweat had blossomed on her skin. His tongue itched to lick her, to taste her, to fucking anything her. He ran a finger up her slit and around her clit before flogging her pussy lightly again.

"Oh!" She cried out this time. "Sir, please!" The last was a drawn-out plea.

"Please what, little one?"

"Please, Sir." She was rolling her head side to side on the pillow as she arched and pumped her hips with each blow and stroke of her slit.

"Tell me what you want, Claire."

"I…don't…know," she huffed between blows. "Just—more! Please!" She screamed the last as the flogger hit her protruding clit. Her honeyed locks were clinging to her face and he could smell her arousal.

His cock was straining against his jeans and he could feel the tip leaking. His own breathing was strained and his heart beat a rapid tattoo as he struggled to contain the raging desire to fuck her hard.

Leaving her pussy, he struck first one nipple then the other, and she screamed with each. She was wild on his bed, writhing and screaming, "Sir! Sir! Oh fuck! Please! Please!"

He continued to stroke her slit in between blows. Her clit was so swollen and her cunt so wet she was soaking the coverlet underneath her. Red stripes covered the creamy mounds of her tits, and her nipples were so distended they looked almost painful.

She continued to scream with each stroke until finally she devolved into an almost mindless chant of "please, please, please."

He reached between her legs and squeezed her clitoris. She broke and so did his control. He ripped open his jeans and pulled out his cock. Flipping her over roughly, he pulled her hips up and impaled her on his shaft.

Her wet, hot cunt was convulsing in orgasm and with the plug in her ass she was unbelievably tight. He began to pound into her. She gloved his cock, squeezing him like a fist. He fucked hard into the velvet heaven of her slick passage, mumbling incoherent words of possession and need.

Gripping her hips, he pounded deeply, bottoming out on her cervix and drinking in her cries of pleasure and ecstasy. His climax rammed into him and he ground himself deep into her cunt, spilling pulse after pulse of hot come in her depths, draining every last ounce of pleasure in her tight pussy.

As his orgasm subsided, he pulled her down with him as he collapsed on his side. The last shudders of pleasure receded and a wave of remorse flooded him, stealing his breath. What had he just done?

Claire struggled to catch her breath in the aftermath of the most intense sexual experience she'd ever had. Small aftershocks wracked her body and she reveled in the knowledge that Evan had finally made love to her. He'd even been chanting "mine" as he'd fucked her hard and deep. It was everything she'd ever hoped it would be.

He was still behind her, joined with her, and she was too overcome to move just yet. He'd not let go of her and she could hear his own ragged breathing that matched her own. She felt full and sated in a way she never had before. Before she was ready, she felt him shift and begin to pull his cock free of her pussy. She clenched instinctively, trying to hold him to her, and smiled softly at his groan, but he prevailed and slipped free of her.

He murmured, "On your belly," and she rolled forward as she realized his intent.

He removed the plug from her ass. She felt the bed shift as he got up and went into the bathroom. She snuggled into his coverlet, thinking back over the experience. The flogging had been unlike what she'd expected. Yes, it had hurt, but the sting had spread out over her skin so that her entire body had felt energized and on fire, but in a good way. When he'd flogged her pussy and nipples it had been so intense she'd been unable to think almost. Each strike to her nipples had been like having a string attached to her clitoris, and she'd felt her pussy pulsing with each blow. By the time he'd actually entered her, she'd been so overwhelmed with pain and pleasure she'd almost willingly have died in that moment.

She heard the water cut off in the bathroom and watched Evan return to her. He still had his jeans on, but his cock was tucked back inside. Only the shadow of his neatly trimmed pubic hair was visible. His flat stomach and lean torso were bare now. He'd been fully dressed while he'd flogged her, but to her disappointment he reached for another T-shirt before coming to sit on the bed beside her.

Something was off. He wasn't looking at her and he wasn't touching her either. This was not exactly how she'd envisioned the aftermath of the first time they made love.

"Evan?" She couldn't keep the tremble out of her voice, but it pissed her off. "Evan, what's wrong?"

He waited so long to reply that she began to believe he wasn't going to answer her at all. When he finally looked at her and spoke, she wished he hadn't.

"I am so sorry, Claire. I shouldn't have done that." He looked ravaged. The lines in his face were deep and his eyes had a haunted look. "I took advantage of you. I broke our agreement. I had no right to do that." He took a deep breath. "I won't do it again. I'm sorry. I just—just can't have this be about sex between us."

Everything inside her went still. The air around her even paused. He was sorry he'd made love to her. *Sorry* that he'd done it. So *sorry* that he was refusing to do it again. Rage flowed through her.

How dare he! How dare he act as if making love to her was wrong? She was not going to stand by and be treated like a mistake.

Oh. Hell. Fucking. No.

She was not doing this. She had more worth than this. Well, fuck Evan and his goddamned dominance. She didn't need this. He could very well go to hell.

Standing, she went into the bathroom and cleaned up quickly before returning to the room and beginning to dress. Evan hadn't moved and was watching her silently. She remained silent lest she rage at him. After all, she had known what she was getting into. She'd agreed no sex. She had not agreed, however, to be insulted like this.

"Claire?" His voice was tentative.

Only when she was fully dressed did she turn to address him.

"Evan." She took a deep breath and looked him square in the face. "We are done." She held up a hand as he opened his mouth to speak. "No. I don't want to hear anything you have to say. You are going to listen to me for a change."

She picked up her purse and put it over her shoulder as she

walked over to where he sat. Reaching out, she stroked his cheek and did her best to memorize the texture of his skin.

"I wanted you to make love to me. I enjoyed it and I would gladly have been in a relationship with you." She dropped her hand. "What I will not be is your guilt trip because you refuse to look inside you and see what the hell has you so scared."

He opened his mouth to speak. "No! Listen." She cut off his objection and he clamped his mouth shut, his face going hard.

"I know you will always love your wife. I would expect no different. But if you really think whatever is going on with you is about loving your wife, you are only fooling yourself. You want me, you've admitted that. This is about fear, Evan. It's obvious to me. Only you are blind to it."

She sighed deeply and stepped back from him.

"Either way, we're done. Your little apology just took one of the most intense and exquisite experiences of my life and tainted it. I am so furious at you right now, I could spit. Thank you, Sir"—there was a sneer in the title—"but I no longer require your services."

She didn't look back as she let herself out and she refused to cry when he didn't try to stop her.

Chapter 15

"Want another, darlin?" Bridget asked.

"Yes, please"—Claire smiled wanly—"and keep 'em coming."

Bridget passed the bowl of mint chocolate chip ice cream to Claire and resumed her seat on the couch.

"I love this scene." Claire waved her spoon in the direction of the TV. "Harry finally admits how he feels about A.J. It's so sweet. All A.J. ever wanted was his approval."

Claire let out a deep sigh.

"I love action movies." She giggled.

They were doing a movie marathon. Currently it was Bruce Willis's *Armageddon*, and next was going to be *Taken* with Liam Neeson. As bad as she felt about what had happened earlier with Evan, she was not going to sulk. No sirree bob, she was not doing it. No sappy romances, no bottles of wine and man bashing. They were, however, having cocktails and lots of ice cream. She was still a woman, after all.

"I love all the sweaty, unclothed men that go with action movies," Bridget said as she licked her own spoon clean before setting her bowl down on the table. "Now, darlin', you know I love you and I respect your privacy, but would you care to clue me into why I canceled study group for an emergency action movie marathon and a gallon of mint chocolate chip?"

Claire watched the credits of the movie for several long moments before finally setting her own bowl down and clicking off the TV with the remote.

Turning to face Bridget, she said, "It's Evan. I told him I never wanted to see him again."

Bridget's face went hard and her voice could have split wood it was so sharp. "Did he hurt you?"

"Oh God no!" Claire cried out and reached for Bridget's hand. "No, babe, he didn't hurt me." She squeezed her friend's hand before setting it down. "Well, at least not the way you mean it."

She picked her ice cream back up and began taking small bites as she talked. "We had a wonderful session together. He was perfect, he introduced me to some things and then"—her face flaming, she glanced quickly up at Bridget—"he made love to me."

"It was amazing, Bridg. Everything I thought it would be and more. It was the single most intense, exhilarating experience of my life. And he absolutely fucking ruined it by being guilty. *Guilty!*" Claire's voice was rising.

"Bridget, I know he loves Marianne. He probably always will, but I don't think this is about that. I think he's afraid of something and he won't face it. That fear is making him keep all this distance between us and I know we could be good together if he would just open his damn eyes and face whatever is scaring him so badly."

"Do you still love him?"

Claire's eyes filled with tears, and she sighed before nodding and saying, "Yes. I wish I didn't right now, but I do. Deeply. I've never connected to another person that way and I've damned sure never entrusted anyone with both my body and psyche that way. But I deserve better, Brig. I won't be his personal guilt trip. I am worth more than that."

Bridget reached out and gave Claire a huge hug. "I love you, darlin', and I'm glad you understand that. You just do what you need to do for you and don't worry about Evan. He's a grown man. He'll take care of himself."

"It still hurts, though, Bridg."

"Of course it does." She released Claire and squeezed her arm. "Love always hurts when it gets off track. But"—she picked up her own ice cream and spooned another creamy bite into her mouth— "that's what sweaty, half-naked men and good ice cream are for!" And she laughed.

Despite all the ice cream, Claire felt warm inside. She'd never had a girlfriend like this before. One she could share with, she could spend time with, and have a girls' night with. Regardless of what had happened with Evan, she was better off for her time at Bibliophile. Her life was irrevocably different.

As that thought resonated in her mind, Claire realized she wasn't going to stop. She would find another dom, but she would be careful about it. You had to be in the BDSM world because mistakes had much more devastating consequences if you weren't.

Settling in for *Taken*, Claire's heart felt lighter after all.

Rolling Hills Memorial Garden had been exquisitely landscaped. The undulating hills that gave the cemetery its name were covered in a verdant carpet that looked soft and ready to roll in. Each plot was neatly landscaped and marked with a flat, engraved stone indicating who lay at rest.

Claire and Chester moved through the rows, searching for the grave they'd come looking for. When she woke up that morning, she'd been filled with the need to visit Marianne's grave. As there was only one cemetery in their tiny university town, she had a good feeling that she'd be lucky and, sure enough, the caretaker had found the plot and given Claire a map with an admonishment to make sure Chester behaved.

They'd found the grave easily enough and Claire had cleared out the drooping flowers that were in the holder inset into the ground. She smiled a bit wryly at the tulips; they were such vibrant, cheery flowers, unlike the elegant, regal calla lilies—her personal favorite—she'd bought on impulse from the little floral shop in the corner of her block. She could imagine Marianne as a tulip girl based on everything she'd heard about her. Claire pulled a few weeds sprouting in the grass and took the debris of her impromptu manicure to the nearby trash can before coming back and facing the grave.

What did you say to a woman you'd never met, and whose widower you were in love with? Claire had no idea, so she figured she'd just have to wing it.

"Marianne, my name is Claire and we never met, but I am in love with Evan." Feeling a little stupid at talking to the air, Claire sat down cross-legged and smiled when Chester moved to sit next to her, leaning his furry body into her, giving her comfort.

A light breeze picked up, stirring the leaves and blowing Claire's hair around her face. Closing her eyes, she inhaled deeply, taking in the scent of earth and sun, before exhaling and proceeding to pour out her heart to a dead woman.

He was going to have to fix that crack. Evan lay on his back in his bed and stared at the offending ceiling. In the days since Claire had left him he'd become intimately acquainted with the shape, texture, and nature of his bedroom ceiling, given how he wasn't sleeping when he was in bed anymore either. He just lay there, staring at the ceiling, kicking himself for being an ass of the worst kind for what he'd done and then, adding insult to injury, torturing himself further by masturbating to the memory of being inside Claire.

He couldn't get her or that day out of his mind, but damn it, he couldn't go there with her. And he'd made that clear from the beginning. She'd called him a coward and what bothered him most was that he hadn't even reacted. Almost as if a part of him knew that what she said was true. Evan had never been a coward in his life; he'd always faced life's challenges head-on, but this—this was something he just couldn't bring himself to do. She'd said he was afraid of something he wasn't facing, but that wasn't it at all. Was it?

He raked a hand through his hair. Whenever he thought of letting go and getting into a relationship with Claire, his stomach twisted in knots and his mind just rebelled at the idea. He was still too much in love with Marianne, that was all. Yes, he wanted Claire and yes, he knew he was being a possessive jerk by enticing her to be his submissive. He just didn't want anyone else initiating her, but that didn't mean he was a coward. A bastard, maybe, but not a coward.

No, she'd done the right thing leaving him. It wasn't fair to either of them, and at least now she'd have a point of reference for what to look for in a dom rather than being completely green. So why did the thought of her with another man still leave him feeling like he could raze the city? *Damn it!* He wished Marianne were there. None of this would be happening if she hadn't left him alone.

On that pained thought, Evan finally succumbed to the pull of sleep and the embrace of his dreams…

"Wake up, love."

Gentle hands stroked his face and brushed his hair back. Everything inside Evan relaxed as Marianne's face came into view. Her lustrous black hair was hanging down her back in an ebony cascade; her face was full and her body lush, just as he remembered her before the cancer.

Wait, how could that be? He clutched her hand and pulled his wife hard into his arms. She felt just as he remembered.

"Mari?"

She tilted her head on his shoulder and pressed a finger to his lips, murmuring, "It's OK, love. It's OK. Just relax and tell me why you called me."

"Called you?"

"Yes, you called out to me and I came because you were hurting so much."

"So this is just a dream?"

She sat up and took his hand in hers, cupping his face. "Yes, baby, but you're hurting and you called for me and I am here. I'll always be here with you. Remember? I promised."

"But you're dead, Mari, and I feel so damned alone without you. You left me and you promised me you'd always stay with me."

A single crystalline tear ran down her cheek. It sparkled so brightly it was almost like diamond.

"I know, baby, but I had no right to make that promise. The universe had other plans for us. I don't have control over that and neither do you. But, Evan, you've forgotten to focus on what we had while we were together. You just torture yourself over what you weren't able to do. You couldn't save me, baby. Nobody could; it was my time."

"Damn it, Mari. I was your dom. It was my job to protect you and I failed you. You died right there in my arms and all I could do was watch you slip away from me. I had to watch. No matter how much I wanted to protect you, wanted to save you, I couldn't…I just couldn't." Evan's voice broke as the grief and anguish he'd held at bay for so long cascaded over him. Sobs rocked his body as all the fear, self-loathing, and recrimination poured out at his inability to do anything other than watch as his beloved wife, best friend, and submissive had died before his eyes.

He felt her stretch out alongside him and wrap him in her arms as he cried. He had no idea how long it was before the tears finally subsided, but he felt like a wrung-out dishcloth. Cool hands stroked his cheeks, wiping away the residue of his grief.

"Evan, look at me, love." His eyes went to her face. "I loved you the best way I knew how and you gave me more love than I knew what to do with. I died happy, in the arms of my husband, partner, and my Sir, and with the knowledge that I had no regrets. What more can a person ask for?

"I want you to be happy, Evan, but you are turning away from a chance at happiness and you aren't even trying to understand."

"I'm afraid, Mari." Shock poured through him as what he'd said registered. Claire had been right; she'd seen right through him.

"I know you are, love, but do you know why?"

He nodded and squeezed his eyes shut before answering, "I'm afraid of losing her too. Of being helpless again."

"That's kind of like not driving a car because you might get into a car accident, don't you think?"

Her matter-of-fact bluntness pulled a bark of laughter from him. That was his Mari. He still missed her.

"I miss you, baby."

She snuggled into him and he held her in his arms, drinking in the feel of her and the spicy scent of her skin.

"Of course you do, I was an amazing woman"—he felt her smile against his neck—"but you are only hurting yourself and another amazing woman you love by acting this way."

Evan stilled at the idea of loving Claire. He had never allowed that thought to even enter his mind, but Mari was right, as usual; he did love her.

"I do love her, Mari, but it's not the same as it was with you…," he rushed to say, but Mari stilled him with gentle lips over his mouth.

"Of course not, love. She's Claire and I'm me and it's okay to love us both for who we are—or were, in my case. You have my blessing, Evan. She seems like exactly what you need. So you are going to have to figure out how to make this right with her." She dropped a light kiss on his neck. "Sleep now, love."

She ran gentle fingers over his eyes, closing them, and blackness overtook him.

―᠆᠆᠆―

Evan woke to golden light pouring into his bedroom. His eyes were crusty with the detritus of his grief, and the details of his dream poured back to him, bringing him to full wakefulness in an instant.

He was in love with Claire and he'd pushed her away. He had to see her and convince her to give him another chance. Throwing back the covers, he headed for the shower.

―᠆᠆᠆―

Evan stared perplexed at the lilies on Marianne's grave. They were fresh and clearly hadn't been there more than a day at most, but who would have done that? Only he ever left flowers at Mari's memorial; neither of them had family in town and the only person he knew of who liked lilies was Claire…

The realization slammed him like a fist in the gut. Claire, it had to have been Claire. Tears welled in his eyes at the image of her leaving flowers for his wife when she believed it was his feelings for Mari driving him to push her away.

Come hell or high water, he was going to get her back. He laid the tulips he'd brought Mari alongside Claire's lilies and said simply, "Good-bye, love, you truly are always in my heart."

Turning, he strode determinedly in the direction of Claire's home.

Chapter 16

SHE WASN'T HOME. *DAMN!* Evan knocked again, hoping against hope that maybe she'd just been in the shower or something and hadn't heard him the first two times. All he got for his effort, though, was the sound of Chester sniffing and mewling on the other side of the door.

Evan rested his head briefly against the door before sighing deeply and resigning himself to being patient. He'd have to try again later. God knew she wasn't coming into Bibliophile anytime soon; she'd made that clear by sending an unsubscribe email to be removed from his mailing list. That had cut, for sure, but he'd haunt her door until she talked to him if he had to.

Turning, he went back down the steps and exited onto the street only to stop short at the sight of Claire and Bridget walking down the street, laden with bags emblazoned with the name of the local lingerie shop. His body quickened at the sight of her. Her petite form was encased in an eggplant-colored T-shirt that hugged her curves and flowed into snug jeans. Her delicate feet were gloved by tall, strappy sandals and it looked like she'd had a pedicure as her nails were painted the same shade as her T-shirt. She was elegantly sexy and her face took his breath away. She was furious and the most beautiful sight he'd ever seen. He loved her. Every cell in his body recognized it, and he'd take her however he could get her, even spitting mad.

"What do you want, Evan?" Her hazel eyes snapped right along with her words as the women drew to a stop in front of him, but he'd seen the way they roamed him first before she caught herself.

"We need to talk." He didn't move or try to touch her, but he looked her square in the eye as he responded.

"I said everything I needed to say to you the other day. Just leave, please." There was a slight hitch on that last word even though she pulled herself together quickly enough.

"I didn't, though. I shouldn't have let you leave that way. Claire, I am asking you to please, just hear me out."

"Why, Evan? So you can convince me to enter back into some sexless and guilt-ridden arrangement with you? I don't think so. I deserve better than that and I'm not settling for being your personal punishment. I won't do it no matter how much you sit here and try to convince me it's for the best or whatever."

She was glorious in her righteous anger. A slight flush on her cheeks, her hands gesticulating, and her hair flowing like a honey waterfall. He wanted to strip her right there on the street and plunge his cock into that smart mouth until he filled it with his come.

"Did you hear me?" She had planted her hands on her hips and was looking at him with narrowed, expectant eyes.

"No." He smiled at her obvious shock. Reaching out, he grabbed her, pulled her hard against him, and kissed her, plunging his tongue inside and exploring her mouth, not relenting until she relaxed against him. Only then did he release her, and as she stood looking both bemused and thoroughly swollen and well-kissed, he said, "I love you, Claire." He took her hand in his and held it gently as he looked into her eyes, now wide with confusion and disbelief. "Please, just hear me out."

Bridget, whom he'd forgotten about, stepped up and hugged Claire, whispering something in her ear before turning and reaching up to drop a kiss on his cheek and say, "It's about time, sugar. Don't fuck up." She smacked his cheek lightly, but grinned wide and sashayed off to her car, leaving them alone.

"Will you hear me out, Claire?" He held his breath, waiting for her reply.

Her eyes welled with tears and she nodded. As he turned to lead the way to her loft, she tugged on the hand he still held and said fiercely when he looked at her, "Don't fuck with my head, Evan. Don't do it. You hear me?"

He saw the fear in her eyes and pulled her in tight, holding her against him and absorbing the feel of her in his arms. Kissing the top of her head, he said, "What was our first rule, baby?"

"Honesty." The word was muffled against his chest.

"That's right, honesty. I will only speak the utter truth to you, and Claire, I love you. Now what we need to do is talk. Will you listen?"

She hugged him so tight that if he'd been a smaller man, she would have squeezed the air right out of him. "Yes."

Pulling away, she took his hand and led him up the stairs, into her home. Evan didn't miss the significance of the gesture.

Claire's heart was obviously determined to take leave of her body. She could feel it galloping its way right up her throat, ready to charge on out the door. She had to take several deep, calming breaths just to make it up the stairs, but she held tight to his hand and tried to control her racing mind.

He loved her! God, she hoped he meant it and wasn't just trying to con her back. She really couldn't handle a mind fuck right now. She'd made up her mind to let him go and continue on with her desires to explore BDSM without him, and now here he was. In a moment of fancy, she'd asked for some sign she was doing the right thing and had come home to find Evan waiting for her.

That seemed pretty damn clear, but if what he had to say wasn't up to her expectations she'd let him go right back out that door too. She wasn't settling. Chester was ecstatic to see her…make that him.

He licked Claire when she knelt to pet him but bypassed her to go to Evan, who he bumped with his big block head and proceeded to follow as Evan took a seat on her couch. Once Evan sat, so did Chester, being sure to lean his big body right up against Evan's leg.

Evan held out his hands to her and said, "Come here, Claire." The implication was obvious that he wanted her in his lap.

"Don't you think that's rushing things a bit?" She kept her face expressionless, but inside her belly quivered.

Evan raised an eyebrow at her and said, "Claire, I've been inside your body. This definitely isn't rushing things. This is making amends. I wanted you in my lap before and I want to hold you and feel you against me now. Will you?" He held a hand out to her, but he wasn't insisting; this was her choice.

She hesitated only a second. She wanted to be in his lap too, and starting off—hopefully they were starting something here—with games served no purpose. She took his hand and settled into his lap, getting a seal of approval from Chester when he licked her ankle. She relaxed into Evan's lean body, enjoying his warmth and the clean, spicy smell of his skin. He hadn't shaved and his face was stubbly. Unable to resist, she reached up and stroked his cheek. He grabbed her hand and kissed her palm before tilting her chin up and leaning down to kiss her again.

His kiss was slow and gentle, as if he were savoring the moment rather than claiming her. He brushed his mouth over hers so softly she almost thought she imagined it before he pressed in deeper. She opened to him, willingly taking his tongue inside her mouth and meeting him in return. He kissed her thoroughly, exploring every cavern and ridge of her mouth, stealing her breath and her heart all over again.

Breaking the kiss, he pulled her in close and pressed her head to his chest. She could hear his heart beating so fast, and she smiled in the knowledge that he was affected too.

"Why?" The question slipped out before she thought, but she let it stand.

He took a deep breath and sighed, picking up a strand of her hair to play with before saying, "I was scared. Mari had been everything to me. My wife, my best friend, my business partner, and my submissive. We had our fair share of bumps, no relationship is perfect, but it was all I ever wanted. When she got sick it was the worst time of my life. I watched the woman I loved so deeply slip away right in front of my eyes and I couldn't do a damn thing about it.

"Do you have any idea what that is like for someone? Especially for someone who practices domination? Every instinct I have is to protect and care for the person I love. That gets exponential when we are talking about my sub, and I was helpless and powerless. I couldn't do anything but stand by and watch."

His voice was harsh and bitter as he spoke, and Claire took his hand and kissed it but didn't stop him. He squeezed her hand in return and she looked up and saw the gentle tenderness in his chocolate eyes as he looked at her.

"That first day you came into Bibliophile, you were so fragile looking. I wanted to scoop you into my lap and have you tell me what was wrong so I could fix it, and that pissed me off more than I can tell you. I hadn't been with anyone since Mari had died and I was content that way. Or so I thought. My dick, on the other hand, was wet and dripping and trying to dance, especially when you called me Sir."

Claire sat up and gaped at him. "I thought you'd been disgusted because I'd been about to come to that story I was reading and you saw me."

He stroked the hair out of her face and tucked it behind an ear. "Nope. I wanted to bend you over my counter and fuck you right there." He grinned at her stupefied expression. "You are one sexy woman, Claire, and you called to all my dominant instincts. I avoided you. Period. I told myself I was still in love with Mari and that I couldn't go there, but then I heard you talking with Bridget about what happened with Charlie and I knew you were ripe for BDSM and submission. The idea of some other guy initiating you made me ill. I rationalized, though, said I would just guide you."

He shifted and pulled her astride his legs so that she was facing him. He rested his hands on her hips and said, "When you agreed to submit to me I continued to rationalize, but I couldn't control myself with you. I wanted you too badly, but I was afraid of losing you. Afraid of being that helpless ever again. So I put in all these rules and boundaries that were bullshit because I just couldn't obey my own rules. I had no right to put that burden on you, baby, and I apologize truly. And I never should have let you leave me, Claire. You are an amazing woman and I love you and I want you by my side if you're willing. I know I screwed up."

Claire's mind was reeling at everything he'd said. He did love her and he was as scared as she was. Taking his face in between her palms, she said, "I'm scared too, Evan." At his raised eyebrow she continued, "I've fucked up every major relationship I've ever had. I have a seriously hard time communicating and I am scared to death I can't live up to what a relationship, especially a relationship like this, needs, but I'm willing and would rather be scared with you than without you." Leaning in, she kissed him softly on the lips and then leaned her forehead against his. "I love you too, Evan."

His grin was wide and open as he caught her to him and hugged her hard. She couldn't contain her laughter at his exuberant response. When he finally released her she sat up and started to stand, only to yelp as Evan scooped her up into his arms.

"What are you doing?" she hollered as he spun her around.

"Bedroom?" He stalked toward the hallway.

She giggled. "Second door on the left."

Chester started to follow them. Evan stopped and turned to look at the dog, saying, "Chester, bed!" Claire was shocked to see her stubborn dog walk calmly over to his bed and drop down contentedly.

She gaped once more at Evan, who grinned at her and resumed his march to her bedroom. "It's all in the tone of voice, baby girl." He kicked the door to her room shut, ensuring they'd remain undisturbed.

With no preamble whatsoever, Evan tossed her on the bed. She bounced once and shouted a laugh as he followed her down and caught her underneath him. One long, heavily muscled leg lay over her own and his warm palm lay on her belly. The look in his eyes dissolved all the breath in her lungs as she watched him lean in and kiss her.

She closed her eyes and savored the kiss. He tasted sweetly of coffee and man and she drank him in. He kissed her as if he had all the time in the world and no plan other than his tongue in her mouth. It didn't take long for the kiss to heat. He nipped at her lips and made love to her mouth the way he would as if it were his cock. She met him thrust for thrust and arched under him as he pressed a powerful thigh between her legs and pressed hard against her crotch.

Claire rubbed against him, enjoying the friction of her zipper against her swelling cunt. Evan stroked her belly, petting her gently for several moments before sweeping the cotton of her T-shirt aside and running his hands over her belly and up to her breasts. He palmed her through the lace of her bra and she savored his moan as he began to squeeze and massage her breast gently.

Ripping his mouth away from her, he jerked up and straddled her body almost frantically, pulling her T-shirt over her head and tossing it on the floor. The sight of him gazing so intently, so lustfully, at her was mind-blowing. Her body reacted violently, drenching her core and tightening her nipples so painfully they stretched the lace of her bra. Evan's face went hard with lust as he ran a fingertip teasingly along the edge of one cup and then pulled the lace down, exposing her flesh. Wetting his finger with his tongue, he traced her nipple, leaving a trail of moisture behind that tingled as it evaporated in the cool air of her bedroom. He repeated the process with her other breast and then reached out to squeeze and tug both of them, eliciting a harsh gasp of pained pleasure from her.

"I've wanted you like this from the start." He growled the words more than spoke them. "Your nipples were so hard that first night in the store, I wanted to rip your shirt off and suck them until you came."

The sheer carnality of his words almost sent Claire over the edge right then and there.

Evan leaned over and said, "I don't want you to speak, Claire. You can moan, you can yell, you can make noise."

He rolled her nipples as he spoke and she moaned and arched into his hands as little shocks ran between her nipples and her clitoris. "But I don't want you to speak. Do you understand, little one?"

She nodded as she bit her lip against crying out his name.

"Good girl." He smiled tenderly. "I'm going to make love to you, Claire. We aren't going to play any real games, but I wouldn't be me if I didn't make you obey somewhat." He punctuated his words with a sharp slap to one nipple and she bucked under him as her pussy flooded and the sting slowly radiated out along her flesh, melting into a slow burn. He slapped her other nipple and she cried out in pain, in pleasure, in desperation for his mouth on her flesh.

"I want to fuck you in every way, Claire. Do you understand?"

She was so caught up in the sting of her nipples and the pulsing in her clit she didn't respond. Evan took both nipples between forefinger and thumb and stretched them taut before letting them snap back. She arched and cried out again. The pressure between her legs was growing and she began to writhe as coils of sensation built in her womb.

Her nipples pulsed and tingled and her clit throbbed. She could hardly concentrate on his words. She felt the edge looming in front of her and knew it wouldn't take much to thrust her over it.

"I want my cock deep in your throat, filling your pussy, and taking your ass. I want it all, Claire. Are you going to give that to me? Give me everything. Let me have you to do with as I please."

Through the haze of her pleasure, Claire sensed this was important that he was asking her to submit to him again, more fully this time, and she nodded at him, remembering not to speak. She looked deep into that beloved, melted chocolate gaze as she did.

The lust and love that flashed across his face stole into her soul. This was what she'd been waiting for. A man who loved her and who would give her what she needed to find fulfillment.

Evan positioned himself between her thighs, spreading her wide to accommodate his body. The pressure of her zipper against her clit became almost unbearable. Evan took one of her distended nipples into his mouth and sucked hard in long pulls before licking her like he was a cat and she the cream. She was fisting the sheets and thrusting rhythmically against him, using his torso as a counterpoint for pressure and friction as the lace of her panties and the rigid zipper of her jeans propelled her higher and higher.

Evan had no mercy on her nipples. He was sucking and biting, licking and laving, tugging and smacking them in turn and it wasn't long before she was screaming and bucking under him as her orgasm consumed her. Ripples of sensation flowed between her sensitized nipples and her distended clitoris. She pulsed and rippled, feeling desperately empty at the same time; she wanted Evan inside her even as she screamed her pleasure.

He had to get inside her. Evan reared up as Claire's orgasm subsided. Unbuttoning her jeans, he peeled them from her body, taking in the wanton sight she made. Her breasts were swollen and flushed from his attentions, the tips hard beads and the tender skin reddened from his spanking. The evidence of her submission to him had his cock dripping and pulsing. She was everything he wanted and he wasn't letting her go again.

The jeans hit the floor, along with the bit of lace passing for panties. He left the bra on. The deep, wine-colored lace—it matched her shirt, he noted—framed her pert breasts and set off the pale cream of her skin. The bra stayed. Evan wasn't nearly so gentle with his own clothes. He was pretty sure he heard a seam rip as he yanked his T-shirt off, and he came very close to catching the cotton of his boxer briefs in the zipper of his jeans because his cock was so damn hard, but he was naked soon enough.

He loomed over her, enjoying how her eyes roamed his body and rested on his cock, which was jutting proudly out from his body. She licked her lips and his cock jumped in response. The slow, sexy smile that played about those luscious lips was enough to tempt him to go straight for her mouth, but he wanted inside her pussy.

Spreading her thighs wide, he knelt between her legs, leaning down and inhaling deeply. Taking in the musky scent of her arousal, mixed in with the sweetly floral scent he'd come to associate with her. She smelled like a woman, his woman, carnal and ready to be owned by him.

Hooking her legs over his shoulders, he wasted no more time in thrusting his cock deeply into her still shuddering cunt. He couldn't contain his groan as her velvet heat closed around him. She was tight and hot and wet and felt so fucking good he almost came right then and there, but he had a goal and he wasn't going to let himself lose it like a teenager who'd never fucked before.

Pulling out almost to the tip, he thrust in hard and deep, enjoying how she arched and writhed beneath him as he possessed her.

"Your pussy is mine, baby girl." To further emphasize his words, he gripped her hips and ground into her, loving the friction of her tightly trimmed thatch against the sensitive skin of his balls. "Mine, and I will use your pussy whenever I want, however I want. Understand?"

"Yes, Sir."

Hearing those words out of her mouth and knowing that she was his and his alone had him fucking hard into her as if he needed to pound her pussy and leave his stamp on her flesh.

He took her legs down, wrapping one around his waist and hooking the other over his arm as he fucked in deep and long. Nipping at her earlobe, he growled, "Say it again."

She wrapped her arms around his neck and met him thrust for hard thrust, squeezing her glorious pussy tightly around his cock, and he groaned as she murmured, "Yes, Sir. I belong to you, love."

His cock went so fucking hard it hurt and he pounded into her pussy, riding the edge of his control. He thrust in deep and hard and held, grinding into her. Her small hands gripped his ass and pulled him in even tighter. He held himself still; he was too close to losing it and he wanted to come in her ass.

He kissed her gently; he'd never thought he'd ever find someone to lose himself with again, and he knew he was doubly blessed to find a woman like Claire. When he had himself back under control, he pulled out and stood by the bed.

"Come here, baby girl. Suck me."

Her eyes flared as she scrambled from the bed, falling gracefully to her knees in front of him. She gripped his rigid shaft by the base and began to lick his cock in long, wet laps. She left no bit of skin untouched as she took every drop of her own juices into her mouth before engulfing his erection and sucking deeply.

He closed his eyes and let his head fall back as the hot suck of her mouth along his throbbing flesh tortured him. It took all of his self-control to remain still and let her have her way with him. He wanted to fist her hair and fuck her mouth. He wanted to pull out and come all over those full lips and watch his fluid spill over her lips and tongue and drip down her throat. He wanted to own her mouth and mark her like a beast.

What he did was hold still and allow her this dominion over his cock. He reveled in the softness of her lips and the gentle tug and pull along his flesh. When she swallowed him down, taking him deeply into her throat, he couldn't hold still any longer. He gripped her hair and began to thrust gently into her wet heat.

Their eyes met; he saw the love and tenderness there and his heart swelled. His woman. He smiled at her and said, "I love you, baby."

Her response was to rub her tongue along the sensitive under-side of his cock and his body went rigid in response. His balls went tight against his body and he again had to stop and pull out to keep himself under control. She was going to test him, that was for sure.

Pulling her up and against him, he held her tightly. She wasn't willing to be still, though, and she began to lick and suck one of his nipples. He groaned and held her head against him, enjoying the sensation of her mouth on his skin and her hand on his cock. She was squeezing and milking his shaft. Little hellion! She wanted him to lose control.

Putting her away from him, he dropped a kiss on her forehead and said, "Hands and knees, baby girl. On the bed." He gave her a gentle push and she complied.

What a sight she made. Her lush ass up in the air, her swollen, red cunt exposed for him to see. Her breasts swollen and her hard, tight nipples jutting out from her body. He stepped up behind her and rubbed her ass lightly. He massaged her hips and legs before cupping her pussy.

Stroking her slit, he dipped into her folds, enjoying the way she clenched around his fingers. Placing one knee on the bed, he leaned over and said, "I told you not to speak, didn't I?"

Her body jolted and she groaned as he lightly smacked her pussy, but all she did was nod.

"You disobeyed me, didn't you?"

Again she jumped and groaned as he smacked her pussy. It was a deep and guttural sound she made, almost animalistic in its quality. He shuddered in response and, moving behind her, thrust deeply into her pussy. He groaned and held himself deeply inside his woman, enjoying the suck and pull of her cunt along his cock. He could live inside her pussy, but it was her ass he wanted today.

He couldn't resist spanking her creamy ass as he fucked her pussy, though, and took an unreasonable amount of pleasure in watching her flesh pink up. She was a fucking dream.

When he pulled out, she whimpered as he left her and his heart swelled even more.

Dipping into her pussy, he coated his fingers with her moisture and inserted them into her ass, scissoring his fingers and stretching her. As he pressed his cock into her anus he murmured, "Push out, baby."

He slipped in, groaning as she clenched against his invasion. Massaging her back, he whispered to her words of love and desire, and she relaxed against him. He pressed in deeper, slipping past the ring of muscle and seating himself deeply in her body.

He stilled to give her time to adjust to him, and just drank in the sight of her sweet ass stretched by his cock, the line of her spine and the cream of her skin still lightly pink from his spanking. To his delight, she began to move first and he joined her rhythm, building slowly to a flashpoint as she gripped and clenched around his cock. His ass and balls were tight and it wasn't going to take much for him to come after denying himself this long.

He fucked her harder and faster, enjoying how she squirmed and moaned as he owned her. She pressed back hard against him, rotating her ass, and he groaned at the way her body pulled and tugged at his cock.

Reaching between her legs, he rubbed her clit as he gripped her shoulder and pounded her hard.

"Come for me, baby. Let me have it."

She gave him everything he asked for. The shudders rolled through her body and she began to convulse around him, screaming mindlessly as she did, pressing hard into his body. He let go and gripped her hips, pounding her hard and slapping her cheeks, savoring the reverberation along his hard shaft as he broke. He hollered her name as his orgasm ripped through him, stealing his breath as he filled her, marking her with his essence.

When he finally subsided, he pulled her down with him to the bed. Sated and replete, he pulled her close and knew he had finally come home.

Epilogue

Six Months Later...

Claire dressed carefully, being certain to follow every instruction to the letter. After hooking the last clip, she inspected herself in the mirror. The red, silk corset hugged her body, nipping in her waist and shaping her breasts. The sheer material of the bodice exposed her nipples while still covering her completely.

She wore silk stockings that were held up by the garter clips hanging from the edge of the corset, and the black leather knee boots hugged her calves while the five-inch heels made her tall and long. She looked like a vixen ready for her man.

Her man...Damn, she still couldn't believe where their relationship had gone over the last six months. Evan had taken her places that she'd never thought she'd go. He pushed her boundaries and explored her limitations, but never once had he gone somewhere she couldn't handle.

She was stronger, more confident, and more in love than she'd ever been in her life. Grinning, she dabbed on the lipstick he loved so much, especially when she left it all over his cock.

Leaving the bathroom, she walked to the center of their bedroom—they'd moved into a new brownstone together just the month before—and took her position on the cushion in the middle of the floor. She knelt demurely, no longer self-conscious in her semi-nude state. With her hands clasped in her lap, she waited.

It didn't take long before she heard him. Her entire body quickened just from the knowledge that he was there. She was tuned to him in a way she'd never been with anyone else. Her nipples went instantly tight and her pussy swelled.

He surprised her, though. Rather than coming to stand before her and offering his cock to suck, he knelt behind her and took her into his arms, wrapping her in a warm, tight hug.

"Claire, I have something special for you tonight. I was going to wait and do something elaborate, but I don't want to wait."

Gripping her shoulders gently, he turned her to face him. Cupping her cheeks, he leaned in and kissed her. Claire's heart leaped in her chest and her breath began to hitch. As he broke the kiss, she roamed his beloved face and waited, not daring to hope.

He stroked her cheek and smiled at her. The love in his face was so profound tears welled in her eyes, which he leaned in and kissed. Releasing her, he reached behind him, and Claire gasped as she saw the red velvet box that was the signature of a local jeweler. As he opened it, she took in the platinum ring that delicately supported the diamond flashing a rainbow of color in the evening light.

Tears flowed freely down her cheeks as Evan smiled at her and said, "Will you marry me, Claire?"

Unable to contain herself, she laughed and cried and said, "Yes."

Grinning, Evan slipped the ring onto her finger. It was a perfect fit.

Acknowledgments

This book could not have been completed without the help and guidance of the kink and BDSM community. You all welcomed me and my persistent questions with patience and open hearts. Thank you all.

I'd also like to thank my family for supporting me in this, my first foray into writing an erotic novel. You kept me on my toes.

Double Time
Sinners on Tour
Olivia Cunning

New York Times and *USA Today* bestselling author

He craves her music and passion

On the rebound from the tumult of his bisexual lifestyle, notoriously sexy rock guitarist Trey Mills falls for sizzling new female guitar sensation Regan Elliott and is swept into the hot, heady romance he never dreamed possible.

She can't get enough of his body

On the rebound from the tumult of his bisexual lifestyle, notoriously sexy rock guitarist Trey's band, The Sinners, Regan finds she craves Trey as much as she craves being in the spotlight.

They both need more...

When Regan's ex, Ethan Conner, enters the scene, Trey's secret desires come back to haunt him, and pleasure and passion are taken to a whole new level of dangerous desire.

Praise for *Rock Hard*:

"Sizzling sex, drugs, and rock 'n' roll...
Absolutely perfect!" —*Fresh Fiction*

"Scorching love scenes...readers will love the
characters." —*RT Book Reviews*, 4 stars

For more Olivia Cunning books, visit:

www.sourcebooks.com

Rock Hard

Sinners on Tour

Olivia Cunning

New York Times and *USA Today* bestselling author

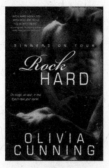

On stage, on tour, in bed, they'll rock your world…

Trapped together on the Sinners tour bus for the summer, Sed and Jessica will rediscover the millions of steamy reasons they never should have called it quits in the first place…

Praise for *Backstage Pass*:

"Olivia Cunning's erotic romance debut is phenomenal." —*Love Romance Passion*

"A sizzling mix of sex, love, and rock 'n' roll… The characters are irresistible. Can't wait for the second book!" —*DforDarla's Definite Reads*, 5 Stars

"These guys are so sensual, sexual, and yummy. This series…will give readers another wild ride…" —*Night Owl Romance*, 5 Stars, Reviewer Top Pick

For more Olivia Cunning books, visit:

www.sourcebooks.com

Wicked Beat

Sinners on Tour

Olivia Cunning

New York Times and *USA Today* bestselling author

How far out are your fantasies?

When Rebeka Blake becomes the Sinners' new soundboard operator, she has no idea that red-hot drummer Eric Sticks is the only man who can give her everything her dirty mind desires…

Praise for *Double Time*:

"Olivia Cunning delivers the perfect blend of steamy sex, heartwarming romance, and a wicked sense of humor." —*Nocturne Romance Reads*

"Snappy dialogue, dizzying romance, scorching hot sex, and realistic observations about life on tour make this a winner." —*Publishers Weekly*

"It just doesn't get any hotter or any better. On- and offstage." —*Open Book Society*

"Smoking hot sex and romance that pulls at your heartstrings." —*Romance Reviews*

For more Olivia Cunning books, visit:

www.sourcebooks.com

Restless Spirit

Sommer Marsden

Three men want her. Only one can truly claim her.

When Tuesday Cane inherits a cozy lake house, she's not expecting to find love as part of her legacy. But how can she choose between Aiden, the loyal and über-sexy handyman she's known for years; the charming and wealthy Reed Green, a former TV star; and the mysterious Shepherd Moore, an ex cage fighter.

The only way to know for sure is to try them all… Surrounded by so many interesting men and erotic temptations, Tuesday has no intention of committing. But deep down she longs for that special, soul-deep connection. Only, which man can entice this restless spirit into finally settling down?

What readers are saying:

"An intense emotional and sexual journey that is quite compelling." —Kathy

"One of the best adult/erotica books I have ever read. The characters are real and believable, and the sex scenes are absolutely scorching hot." —Rebecca

"Themes of domination and submission are fantastically well varied throughout the story… Realistic and relatable characters with steamy encounters at every turn." —Michelle

For more Xcite Books, visit:

www.sourcebooks.com

Control

Charlotte Stein

Will she choose control or just let go?

When Madison Morris wanted to hire a shop assistant for her naughty little bookstore, she never dreamed she'd have two handsome men vying for the position—and a whole lot more. Does she choose dark and dangerous Andy with his sexy tattoos? Or quiet, serious Gabriel, whose lean physique and gentle touch tempt her more than she thought possible?

She loves the way Andy takes charge when it comes to sex. But the turmoil in Gabe's eyes hints at a deep well of complicated emotions locked inside. When the fun and games are over, only one man can have control of her heart.

What readers are saying:

"Forget Fifty Shades of Grey...take a look at this
and see how long you can stay in control!"

"This is honest to god, hands down, the
best erotic fiction I've ever read."

"Highly addictive!"

For more Xcite Books, visit:

www.sourcebooks.com

The Initiation of Ms. Holly

K. D. Grace

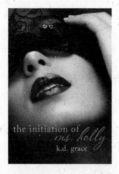

The stranger on the train

He came to her in the dark. She couldn't see him, but she could feel every inch of his body against hers in the most erotic encounter Rita Holly ever had. And now he's promising more…if she'll just follow him to an exclusive club where opulence and sex rule. She can have anything she's ever dreamed of—and more—but first she'll have to pass the club's initiation…

What readers are saying:

"After reading *Fifty Shades of Grey*, I didn't think I would find another book as well written, but then I read *The Initiation of Ms. Holly*, and I was immediately taken in. This book is sexy, erotic, and explosive. I didn't want to put it down." —Dani

"Very, very erotic and sizzling!!! Wow, I could not put it down." —Theresa

"Everything you want in a romantic, erotic, sexual novel." —Jean

"For a fast-paced read with enough twists and turns to keep the story fresh and entertaining, you couldn't ask for a better book." —Christine

For more Xcite Books, visit:

www.sourcebooks.com

In Your Corner

Sarah Castille

Coming Spring 2014

A high-powered lawyer, Amanda never had any problem getting what she wanted. Until Jake. She was a no-strings-attached kind of girl. He wanted more. Two years after their breakup, she still hasn't found anyone nearly as thrilling in bed. And then he shows up in her boardroom…

Jake is used to fighting his battles in a mixed martial arts ring, not in court. He needs Amanda's expertise. And whether she knows it or not, she needs him to help her find true happiness.

Praise for *Against the Ropes*:

"Smart, sharp, sizzling and deliciously sexy.
Against the Ropes is a knockout."
—Allison Kent, bestselling author of *Unbreakable*

For more Sarah Castille books, visit:

www.sourcebooks.com

Against the Ropes

Sarah Castille

He scared me. He thrilled me. And after one touch, all I could think about was getting more...

Makayla never thought she'd set foot in an elite mixed martial arts club. But if anyone needs a medic on hand, it's these guys. Then again, at her first sight of the club's owner, she's the one feeling breathless.

The man they call Torment is all sleek muscle and restrained power. Whether it's in the ring or in the bedroom, he knows exactly when a soft touch is required and when to launch a full-on assault. He always knows just how far he can push. And he's about to tempt Makayla in ways she never imagined...

Praise for *Against the Ropes*:

"Smart, sharp, sizzling, and deliciously sexy." — Alison Kent, bestselling author of *Unbreakable*

For more Sarah Castille books, visit:

www.sourcebooks.com

About the Author

Hailing from Washington, D.C., Elene Sallinger first caught the writing bug in 2004 after writing and illustrating several stories for her then four-year-old daughter. Her writing career has encompassed two award-winning children's stories, a stint as a consumer-education advocate, as well as writing her debut novel, *Awakening*—a novel of erotic fiction that won the New Writing Competition at the Festival of Romance 2011.